# The

## Chris Miller

Copyright © 2019 by Chris Miller
All Rights Reserved

ISBN: 978-1-950259-06-9

0000-0614-0000

www.deathsheadpress.com

Cover by Becky Narron and Don Noble

*For A. M.*

*You silence my demons*

# Foreword
The Worst is Also the Best
by Mark Deloy

I've been thinking about bad guys lately. I've been thinking about the villains, the fiends, the darker lot of us, the ones who refuse to play by society's rules yet still somehow capture our imaginations and, in many cases, end up winning the day.

It's sometimes difficult to quantify exactly who a villain is. Yes, they do bad things, but much of the time it's to advance their goal, get ahead, or, as I mentioned above, to win. This is something we are all guilty of. We sometimes go against the grain, do something sneaky—or even illegal—to advance our inner hero's progress toward the end-game. We look at a situation, determine the desired outcome, sometimes weigh the risks (sometimes not), then we fucking go for it.

Yes, there are the straight arrows who do play by rules and always try to do the right thing, but most of us have done something we aren't particularly proud of, but know it will get us ahead. It's human nature, especially in this cut throat world where you see memes on Facebook that preach "be nice to everyone because you don't know what they've been through" or to "always be kind". But you and I know what life is really like, down where it's dark, down where you make decisions to survive, and sometimes those decisions hurt others. It's wrong, and it sucks, but it's the truth.

This is why I think we as a society are obsessed with bad guys. We love to hate them, yet still love them a little, because deep down we know at least some part of them is us.

This isn't a modern phenomenon either. Of course, the earliest and the worst villain in terms of being a complete polar opposite of God was Satan, but even he has some qualities that make you (pardon the pun) warm up to him. He was once a good guy, in fact, he was the most beautiful of all God's angels, but in typical bad guy fashion, he wanted more for himself. You can perhaps compare him to a much more recent villain, Jame Gumb, aka, Buffalo Bill. They both coveted something. For Satan, it was to be greater than God. For Bill, it was to have smooth skin. We all have our kinks.

Shakespeare had terrific villains. Iago hates Othello so much that he convinces him that his wife is having an affair with Othello's lieutenant. Iago possesses a quality akin to many other bad guys. He's not physically formidable or dangerous looking, but he's smart, manipulative, cunning, and willing to take a chance to get what he wants.

One of my favorite literary villains for the same reason is Professor Moriarty from Sherlock Holmes. As brilliant as Holmes was, Moriarty's intellect rivaled his own. Holmes called him the "Napoleon of crime", and in one case describes him as "crime itself." A fitting arch nemesis for the world's greatest detective, aside from Batman of course.

And speaking of Batman, I'll bet you instantly thought of the Joker. Yes, Batman has had all types of weird, wacked out cronies to contend with, the Penguin, the Scarecrow, but who killed Robin? Who gassed David Letterman's entire audience until they died with a smile on their faces? That's right, the clown prince of crime. I can remember watching Heath Ledger play the Joker in movie, The Dark Knight. I watched the screen, begging for the next scene in which he would appear. I did the same thing when I watched Silence of the Lambs waiting for Hannibal to speak the lines pulled straight out of Thomas Harris's masterwork. Yes, Clarice was a terrific character as well, but Hannibal Lecter was the main draw and still stands as my favorite villain of all time. Now think about that for a minute. My favorite bad guy—no actually, my favorite character in literature—is a cannibal, perhaps the worst thing you can be as a human being. That's the power of an author. To take the worst of the worst and make you love them.

Women make especially good villains. Who can forget Annie Wilkes from Stephen King's Misery, or one of my earliest childhood terrors, The Wicked Witch of the West.

A more recent addition to villainesses that will go down in fame is Harley Quinn. Margot Robbie was as beautiful and sexy as she was crazy and homicidal in Suicide Squad. Female baddies are especially enduring because from the minute we are born, we look to females as the ultimate good, the nurturers and the comforters. Then you pick up Harry Potter and the Order of the Phoenix and encounter Delores Umbridge, and all that loving, nurturing warmth goes away, and you wish you could strangle a character through the pages.

Even real-life bad guys garner fame and in some cases adoration. Ted Bundy ended the lives of 30 women and girls, yet received fan letters and nude photos from several women, even marrying one of them. Carol Ann Boone, one of Bundy's rabid female supporters, ended up marrying him while testifying on his behalf as a character witness. Bundy proposed to Boone in the middle of questioning her as his own attorney. Boone accepted, and Bundy said, "I do hereby marry you." According to media sources, Boone had contacted a notary public to attend the trial, and their marriage was later pronounced legal.

The fun newish term for bad guys now—mostly thanks to Deadpool's success—is the anti-hero. It's best described by its Webster's definition: "A central character in a story, movie, or drama who lacks conventional heroic attributes." I suppose that's so we don't feel bad about liking the character, and it works. Well, why? Again, it's because we see their flawed nature and draw a comparison to ourselves. We realize that we all strive to be better, and often times, we fail. And that's okay. It makes the world go round.

You are about to dive into Chris Miller's *The Hard Goodbye*. Chris has a way of pulling you into the worlds he creates and then shutting off the lights. He wants you to feel as if you belong there in the dark with him, and you do. Deep down, you like it there. It feels like home. I have no doubt that you will love his characters. I did. Why?

Because they are really bad.

Mark Deloy, author of *The Southern House*
2019

# Chapter 1

When the spike was first driven through Larry's foot, he was convinced he'd reached an exquisite level of pain which couldn't be topped.

He soon found this to be incorrect.

A mangled, shouting whimper tore from his throat as spittle and snot sprayed the big guy in front of him holding the hammer. Larry could hear bone and sinew cracking and snapping as his foot tried to move involuntarily, and fresh pain exploded up his body. He began to shake. Fast, hitching breaths heaved from his mouth around his gritted teeth.

*Oh, Jesus,* Larry thought. *Oh, God, what have I gotten in to?*

The swell of pain began to subside slightly, moving out like a tide. It would be back, he knew, like all tides. But if he could just keep his foot still, he thought the pain could be tolerable.

He winced again and his eyes fluttered open through matted lids. Blood and tears were caked around his sockets, but he could still see okay. The big guy was on one knee in front of him, the hammer still in his hand, a look of total indifference on his face. There was another guy standing to the side, his right hand clasped over his left wrist. He was sporting a similar look to the man in front of him. They were just there. They had no malice in their eyes at all, only a look of waiting. Waiting for the third man's next order.

Larry shifted his gaze then and his eyes met the third man's. They were black. Devoid of conscience. Devoid of humanity. There was nothing in them, yet they seemed to blaze in a dark fire. There was no hate there, much like the other two men. Unlike the other two men, this one seemed to be enjoying this. It was the most frightening thing about him. The utter lack of anything resembling emotion. Hate was a human thing. It was tangible. You could understand it, wrap your mind around it. But this was like looking into an alien thing, something from another world, another dimension, a thing which considered human life as...as what?

No. It didn't consider human life at all. That was the terrifying part. The indifference. The inhumanity.

Larry Horowitz didn't want to look into those eyes, but he found himself unable to pull his gaze away. His own eyes were pained, swollen from the beating he'd taken so far, still straining to create imperfect *ohs* of horror. But as the eyes continued to bore into him, he dug deep and found what was left of his backbone and used it like a crutch as he set his lips hard, his jaw muscles bulging.

"I'll ask again," the man who seemed to be enjoying this said. "Where is it?"

Larry managed a soft chuckle which turned to a sharp wince as his foot tried to shift and his instep bellowed in protest. He drew in a deep breath and set his face once more.

"Fuck you," Larry said.

A hint of something which could have been the beginnings of a smile seemed to crease the man's skin just over the corner of his mouth, but it quickly vanished.

"Never heard of the place," the man said, a look of mock curiosity suddenly shadowing his face. "Is it near here?"

Larry's face must have betrayed his wonder, because the man began to laugh, his two pals joining in. He was *joking*? Now? Larry was taped to a chair, his face bloody and beaten, a fucking railroad spike pounded through his left foot, and the man was making jokes?

The laughs stopped as suddenly as they'd begun, and the man jutted his chin towards the man on the floor. A second later, the hammer was coming down again on the spike and Larry knew he'd only just waded into the shallow end of pain.

He screamed as the hammer fell three more times on the spike, the last strike jumping off the spike's head and smashing his large toe. From the initial squashing sound, Larry was sure it had just turned to a sort of paste inside his shoe. Like something served on crackers to rich snobs at parties with cool jazz playing somewhere in the background.

The pain was absolute. Larry gasped. He cried. Tears spilled over his cheeks.

"I don't know!" he managed to shout between agonized cries. "I don't know where it is!"

"Well, that's what they all say," the man said with a shrug. "At first, that is. Eventually, the story changes. It always does. Like a rewrite. You know what a rewrite is, Larry?"

Through the pain and tears, Larry looked at the man incredulously.

"W-wha—"

"It's when a writer—could be the author of a novel, or a screenwriter, it's essentially the same all around—when he finishes typing out his story he knows it isn't actually finished. He looks it over and he realizes it's shit. All first drafts are shit, Hemingway said so. And generally speaking, he was right. So, the writer takes the shit he just wrote, and he starts revising it. A little rewording here, cutting utter crap out there, and so on. Maybe he fleshes some things out. Adds more details, puts some more meat on the bones. Puts in some backstory."

"I-I don't..." Larry began and trailed off, shaking his head.

"Point is, Larry," the man went on, "every good story you've ever read, every good movie you ever watched, it went through a rewrite. Probably more than one. Because if you just hammer out the first thing that comes to you and throw it out there for the world to see, they'll throw it back in your face. That's the part we're at right now. Throwing it back in your face."

He did the thing with his chin again and the man on the floor obliged with another indifferent whacking with the hammer. Larry swam deeper into the swamp of pain, dredging new depths. His cries turned to whimpers, and the man let him cry. The look on his face told Larry he believed he had earned his cry. He was in a swamp of pain and a sea of terror already, but the look the man was giving him now threatened to tear at the seams of his sanity.

"Rewrite the script, Larry," the man said and clapped his hands. The sound cracked in the room. "Give me something I can publish."

Larry grimaced, his lips peeling back over his gore-streaked teeth, and spat. The effect was diminished, though, because the gob of bloodied spittle barely cleared his chin. It splatted to his shirt and vanished among the rose blossoms of blood smattering it.

"You can do better than that," the man said.

*Was that another joke?* Larry wondered. He thought it was, but he couldn't be sure.

The man leaned back against the corner of Larry's desk and pulled a pack of cigarettes out of his jacket. He chose one from his pack, put it between his lips, and lit it. The pack and lighter vanished back into his jacket.

"Tell you what, Lar," the man said as he took a long drag on his cigarette and blew the smoke out into the room. "You mind if I call you Lar?"

He pronounced it *Lare*. Larry only stared at him.

"A little incentive. It always helps me give it all I've got when I've got some skin in the game. Gives me that extra little push I need to get the job done."

Larry began laughing out loud now, and this time he was able to ignore the rhapsody of pain cascading up his leg. The guffaws were deep and genuine.

The man continued to stare at him indifferently.

"In-incentive!" Larry said through continued barks of laughter. "What the fuck do you think you can incentivize me with? I'm already a dead man, you think I don't know that? I may not be the brightest guy, but I'm no fool. Fuck your incentive and just get it done!"

Another chortle leaped from his mouth, but then he fell silent.

The man drew on his cigarette again, then stood and put his free hand in his pocket. He stood there like that, and Larry thought he looked like a man standing on a street corner waiting for the light to change.

"Where's Brenda, Lar?" the man finally asked.

All traces of laughter were gone in an instant as though being sucked out of him into the vacuum of space.

"W-what do you—"

"Come on, Lar, you know what the fuck I mean. Where is she?"

Larry's wife had taken their son, Dylan, to see her parents that afternoon. They had planned to stay overnight, but he realized now he hadn't heard from her. She was supposed to call when she got there, to let him know they'd made it okay. What time would they have been there? Five, maybe five-thirty? He looked to the clock on the wall and saw it was well past nine, and these men had only been here for an hour or so. She should have called. Hell, *he* should have called, but he'd let himself get busy with the work he had piled on his desk and hadn't bothered.

*Why hasn't she called?*

"What have you done?" Larry asked in a wavering voice which betrayed any trace of bravado he may still have had.

The man's face cracked open in a smile and he took another drag from his cigarette.

"Did she take the boy with her, Lar?"

New species of fear stole through Larry like centipedes, crawling over his flesh, which now mounded with goose-pimples.

"What have you done with them?!" he bellowed, indignant rage boiling through him, fueled by the fresh terror.

The man shrugged. "I'm just curious, Lar, honest. Nice house, nice family, good looking kid. How old is he?"

Larry's face rippled and flushed, but he was unable to speak.

"Be a shame to lose things so...precious, wouldn't it, Lar?"

"God-damn you," Larry hissed. "If you lay a hand on either one of—"

"Rewrite, Lar," the man said, cutting him off. "Give me a rewrite I can sell, then we'll talk about your family."

"Please!" Larry begged, "I can take care of it! I can fix it!"

Larry was screaming the words, though he wasn't aware of it. His wrists and ankles worked against the duct tape, and he was only faintly aware of the pain in his foot now. But the tape didn't give and the spike stood defiantly from his foot, rendering him immobile and helpless.

*"PLEASE!"* Larry continued to scream. "I can make a few calls! It will be taken care of by morning *at the latest*, I swear! J-just, please, don't hurt them!"

As if to punctuate this last part, the giant goon in the corner—who'd been mostly docile up to this point—moved toward him fast, shooting his massive hand out like a rocket. It smashed into Larry's nose with colossal force. Skin split and cartilage shredded. There was a wet crunch and Larry screamed again, this time more hoarsely. Blood jetted from his nose, spritzing his shirt in dime-sized drops.

"Rewrite the story, Larry," the man with the cigarette repeated.

Larry peered through a scarlet filter as blood streaked his face, looking down now after the blow, away from those black, indifferent eyes. He noticed the blood was getting into the carpet. A large pool of it had already collected on the floor to his left, around his ruined foot. He'd just had the goddamned carpet shampooed not even a week ago and now it was stained—likely irreparably—with his blood.

*That'll be a bitch to clean,* he thought absurdly, and nearly burst out with an insane bark of laughter, one he barely contained. Instead he winced at the sharp pain in his nose, his foot, everywhere.

The man stepped forward and Larry looked up to him again. The cold, indifferent eyes were still there, unblinking. The cigarette hung from the man's mouth, tendrils of blue smoke coiling into the air, thinly veiling his fierce, hard face. As Larry watched, the man took a drag on the cigarette and pulled it away from his mouth, pinched between his index and middle fingers, sucking in a gulp of air through pursed lips. The man smiled almost imperceptibly as he exhaled the smoke. It came out in thick, white and blue ropes as he moved closer. It occurred to Larry that the smoke almost seemed to be coming from *within* the man rather than from the cigarette. There was so god-damn much of it. Like there was some unquenchable fire burning inside him. As if Hell itself burned inside the man's chest.

The man leaned down close to Larry's face, staring at him intently. His face was leathery and hard, wrinkled here and there with age and smoke, though he wasn't an old man. He was a hard man. An unflinching man.

When he spoke this time, all of the playful banter was gone. It was a voice so deep and intimidating it seemed almost inhuman.

"All I want is a location," the man said. "Not a name. Not a personal description. You don't have to have their faces on your conscience at all. I can handle the rest. Just tell me where to start, and I'll handle the rest."

The man's hard face split into a smile which could almost be interpreted as warm. His tobacco-stained teeth glistened.

"Just a location," he went on, the warmth of his voice undercut by an icy river of indifference beneath the surface. "If you can do that for me, it will be quick. I can promise you that. And you won't have to worry about your family."

Now the man stood fully erect, the hand holding the cigarette flipping to the side in a shrug as his eyebrows rose.

"If you can't do that for me," the man went on, his smile vanishing, "well..."

He paused for a moment. Whether it was for effect or to search for the words, Larry didn't know, but it sent cold shivers down his spine all the same.

The man locked eyes with him again and took another long drag on his cigarette before continuing.

"Well, then, I won't let you die. And Dylan, well, I'm sure you don't want to explore the possibilities there. Or your wife's sweet little ass."

Cold terror locked Larry's breath in his lungs, catching it about his throat as the man's steely eyes bore into him.

"W-what about the others?" Larry asked, blubbering now. "They're my friends, for fuck's sake! I-If I tell you, would you—*will you*—promise me no one will be hurt? There's no reason to go after them or my family. I know where it is, you can just take it!"

"The only person who'll be hurt is you, Lar," the terrifying man said flatly, but not without compassion, feigned or not. "Only you."

Larry swallowed hard, his throat clicking audibly, and began to nod slowly as he sniffled, trying to get his sobbing under control.

He told the man everything. In spite of the man's request for only a location, Larry seemed to develop a bad case of diarrhea-of-the-mouth as he began telling the man his story. The man didn't stop him. He simply stood there quietly, his eyes fixed on Larry, casually smoking one cigarette after another.

Larry gave the man the location. He gave the man names. Descriptions of each of them. Even phone numbers. The whole spiel took about six minutes to finish. By the end, the man was smiling widely, his yellowed teeth exposed.

"You've done good, Lar," he said as he crushed out another cigarette on the desk.

He pulled a black .45 automatic out of his suit coat, pulled the slide back, and let it slam shut. The metal chinked and chimed as a round seated into the chamber.

"Very well indeed."

"W-What's going to happen to them?" Larry asked, a stupid look of pleading spreading on his face as he realized all he'd just spilled to the man. It was a pointless question now.

The man exhaled an exasperated sigh. "Nothing they don't deserve."

He paused and chuckled. More of a humorous grunt, really.

"Well...maybe just a *little* more than they deserve."

This brought laughter from the man's two goons. Larry realized how idiotic the term *goons* seemed to him, though he'd only thought it, not spoken it aloud. He almost laughed himself at the thought, though as fresh pain swelled through the bridge of his ruined nose and foot, the reality of his situation came crashing down on him, crushing all humor under its weight.

*Why'd you do it, Larry?* an inner voice asked him. *You gave him everything. You god-damned coward.*

Tears streaked out of Larry's eyes even as he tried to reason with the accusing voice in his head. The man would have found out anyway. He'd made that clear. So why not give him the location, and names and numbers and descriptions? Why not just give him everything?

"Y-you promised no one would get hurt," Larry whimpered. "You promised they—"

"I lied," the man cut him off with a shrug. Then his face took on an *oh, yeah* quality and the first finger of his free hand went up. "Almost forgot these."

His hand snaked into the pocket of his jacket and pulled two items out. Larry recognized them at once, and his bowels turned to water and evacuated.

The man tossed the first item onto his lap. It was a paracord bracelet. A small one, made for a child. He knew this, because he'd made this very one with Dylan over the summer. Horror began to well in his guts and now his bladder betrayed him and let go. He sat there in his own excrement, a horrified moan spilling from his mouth as his bloodied eyes bulged in their sockets.

The man tossed the second item onto his lap.

"Thought you might want these," the man said, and he and the other two men began to bellow with laughter.

The second item was his wife Brenda's wedding ring. This was bad enough, but what really sent Larry's horror into the stratosphere was her finger, still inside the ring, a red stump protruding out one end.

Larry's moan reached a crescendo and he began wailing and screaming incoherent, garbled nonsense. The three men continued to laugh at him, the big guy from the corner wiping errant tears from the corners of his eyes. The abject horror of his situation seemed surreal to Larry now, and the cackling laughter of the monsters in his study added a fresh level of absurdity to the moment, one almost as horrible as the realization that his wife and child were dead. Murdered at the hands of these barbarians.

The laughter continued, but the man holding the silenced .45 added one more bit of information, fleshing out the details in the final rewrite to the sad end of the Horowitz family.

"Your wife's ass really is sweet," he said, still laughing. "What's that tattoo on her right cheek? Was that a spade?"

Larry hitched another breath and began to scream again, more pitifully now. The men continued to laugh at his misery, like vampires feeding on blood.

He'd just gotten them all killed. All sent into the great beyond, or whatever there was. His wife, his boy. His friends would be next, he knew.

*You god-damned coward.*

The laughing stopped, and Larry's screaming was reduced to no more than a strained, hoarse whisper. Even this finally died down as Larry stared at his wife's finger and his son's bracelet. He wanted to cry some more, he *needed* to, his family deserved it, but there were just no more tears in him anymore.

Finally, Larry looked up to the man. The man stared into his eyes, and a smile which could only be described as satanic split his face. Larry looked about the room at them, his view little more than a reddish blur now. Guilt welled within him, an almost sickening tide. He had sold out his friends for a quick and easy death, and the sparing of the lives of his family. He'd even spilled far more than he'd needed to, more than he'd meant to. It had just flowed out of him, the words greased with the hope of self-serving cowardice. But he'd been unable to stop it, no matter how much he may have wanted to. One look into the man's dark eyes and Larry knew he was deadly serious about what he'd said. And, of course, the man had been lying. All lies meant to draw out of Larry the information he wanted. All god-damned lies.

*I won't let you die. And Dylan...your wife...*

Those words echoed in Larry's memory, bouncing back, then ebbing out again off the dark stone corridors in his mind, welling from an inky abyss.

The room was eerily silent now, only the sound of their breathing and the soft crackle of the man's fresh cigarette smoldering as it hung from his lips. Larry drew in a deep, rasping breath and made an attempt to sit up straight in the chair. He couldn't do it. His head was swimming with pain, dread, guilt, despair. He simply could not sit himself up. Instead, he tried to look the man in the eyes, though it was very hard with the blood in his own.

"W-who are you?" Larry asked the man in a pitiful groan. He was shivering.

The man's smile faded as he raised the gun to Larry's head, blowing out smoke as he drew the cigarette away from his lips.

"Call me Mr. Spears."

Larry saw the flash of the pistol and his world went black barely a moment later. The man had at least kept one of his promises to Larry.

It was quick.

## Chapter 2

John Savage reached into his pocket and dug out his key. After opening the front door to his ground level, two story condo, he reached around behind him, grabbed two duffel bags, and brought them inside. He smiled at their weight and, when he dropped them to the floor near the closet, his ears were met with a satisfying *thump*.

"Jenny? Jen, you home?" he called out.

He was an average sized man of thirty-three years. His jet-black hair hung tousled about his face, and he ran his fingers through it to get it out of his eyes as he let out a tired sigh. He wore a sleeveless undershirt beneath a black leather jacket and a pair of worn blue jeans. His boots clunked along the faux hardwood flooring of the downstairs living area, and the sound brought to mind one of the few memories he had of his father when he'd come home from working construction in the Dallas area, clomping along his way to the first place he went every day when he came through the door after quitting time.

The refrigerator.

John headed to his own now, opening the door and snatching up a bottle of Lone Star—his father's brand, if memory served—and cracked the top off with the side of the counter. He drank deep, though it was still early, chasing a threatening hangover back to whatever hell it came from.

He sighed with satisfaction as he finished a gulp and let the fridge door fall closed behind him as he moved back towards the living room. He thought of his dad as he went, shaking his head and taking another pull on his beer.

Mike Savage had set out one night after finding the last beer in the fridge at about 8 P.M., declaring he was heading to get a refill and a pack of smokes. That was the last time either John or his mother had seen the man, John reckoning the pack of cigarettes the man was after must have been an elusive brand, since he was still out looking for them. John had been ten years old.

John grew up in Dallas until he was thirteen, when his mother had moved them to Winnsboro, a small town about a hundred miles east of Big D where she had an aunt they were able to move in with, and his formative years and beyond had been spent there.

It was in Winnsboro where he had met Jenny at the age of twenty-three, at a bar called 'Triple D Saloon'. It was a decent dive, at least for the area, and it was the place where all the locals gathered to gossip about their neighbors, drown their sorrows, or watch sports— namely football—on any one of the four big screens hanging from the walls. Other sports were shown there as well, and some of the folks would lay down cheap, twenty-or-so dollar bets from time to time for fun. This was technically illegal, but no one seemed to mind, and there were no shylocks roaming the streets breaking knees to collect if someone welched. Harmless, small-town stuff.

He'd nuzzled himself up to the bar, ordering the Savage special—a Lone Star beer and a shot of Jack Daniel's—and was taken as a gorgeous woman stepped up to the bar next to him ordering a vodka gimlet. His jaw must have been somewhere near the floor, because the lady had noticed him and blushed as she chuckled.

"Take a picture, honey, it'll last longer," she had said to John, who immediately felt his jaw snap shut with an audible click.

"I-I'm sorry," he had stammered, desperate to save face. "You just remind me of someone."

"Is that right?" she said as she turned her back to the bar and sipped her gimlet.

John had laughed, a hint of his confidence coming back to him now.

"Yeah, sorry about that."

There was a moment of what should have been awkward silence which passed between them, but oddly enough, it hadn't been. John marveled at her beauty, more subtly this time, and wondered just how old she was. She couldn't be any older than he, and he doubted she was even that. She was young, but the bartender hadn't given her a second look when he served her the drink. Maybe she came in here regularly, he thought, but he couldn't imagine that he'd have missed a beauty like this.

She was staring over his shoulder now, and her eyes brightened.

"My team's playing tonight," she said.

John glanced over his shoulder at the TV on the wall and saw the Cowboys and Packers had just kicked off. He smiled and looked back to her, taking a drag on his beer.

When he finished his gulp, he said, "Mine too. Cowboys are gonna tap that ass."

She had laughed, almost choking on her drink.

"Ha! That'll be the day!"

John remembered the abject, horrified astonishment he'd experienced at her statement. They were, after all, deep in Cowboys territory, and rooting for any other team was akin to molesting a statue of the Blessed Virgin Mary.

"Hold up," John had said, raising a hand. "You're a Packers fan? You're not from around here, are you?"

But even as he said this, he was sure she was. The accent placed her squarely in East Texas, he was positive.

"Born and raised, honey," she said and winked at him.

John shook his head in disbelief. "Well, darling, you're gonna get the disappointment of a lifetime tonight. Dallas is going to spank Green Bay. You can take that to the bank."

She smiled and leaned in close to him.

"Care to put your money where your mouth is, hotshot?"

He had blinked, but then she was slapping twenty dollars down on the bar in front of him and betting him that the Packers would beat the Cowboys by seven. A prideful young man, and loyal to his boyhood home team, he had laughed at her, producing his own twenty.

"Okay, okay," he said stacking his cash on top of hers, "I'm game. But don't say I didn't warn you."

Dem 'Boys were up all the way through the third quarter, at which point he'd asked her if she wanted to back out on their bet.

"No hard feelings," he had said, sipping at his beer. "I'll cut you some slack, since you obviously have poor taste in football."

Her eyes had thinned in playful indignation. "You think so, huh?"

"I know so, darling. Who the fuck would bet against America's team, anyhow? What are you, a socialist?"

They shared a laugh at this, then her face went serious and she leaned in close again. This time he could smell her perfume, faint in the boozy aroma of the bar, but there, and wonderful. Lilacs, he had thought, and would later find he had been right.

"Double or nothing," she said, slapping another twenty on the bar atop their pile.

John had looked at the fresh bill, the neck of his bottle still touching his lips, and felt a flush of heat blossom in his cheeks. She was a ballsy broad, he had to give her that. But he liked her. Socialist or not, she was definitely his type, and he meant to see this through. After all, good-old American capitalism was built on risk, wasn't it? Not that there was much risk here, dem 'Boys were about to embarrass those ass-Packers all over live television.

He wasn't about to back down now. He had set his bottle down, smiling broadly and nodding slowly.

"Alright," he had said. "You have bad taste in teams *and* you need to learn a few things about playing the odds. Good thing I'm a professor in these fields. Happy to teach you a lesson."

He had slapped a second twenty down on top of hers with an arrogant smile and wink of his eye, knowing he would buy her as many drinks as she wanted to pay her back—he wasn't a vindictive man—but she was about to get a lesson in gambling she wouldn't soon forget.

By the end of the night he had lost his bet with her–but he *had* gotten her phone number and her name. It was Jenny. He supposed that was sufficient recompense for his humiliation—and never mind that of the Cowboys, what an abysmal fourth quarter *that* had been—and he'd gone home that night with a smile on his face. Now, ten years later, he stuck his head up the staircase to call out to her again.

"Jenny?"

He listened a minute more before noticing he could hear the shower going upstairs and realized where she was.

He made his way up the stairs and headed into their bedroom, which was across the hall from the shower. He drank the last gulps of his beer down, set it on the dresser, and belched. As he pulled his jacket off and tossed it onto the bed, he heard the water turn off in the bathroom. He kicked his boots off and sat on the end of the bed, leaning forward to rub his feet. About the same time he did this, he heard the bathroom door open.

"Hey, did you get in touch with Larry?" John asked absently as he massaged his toes. "I tried calling him earlier but—"

He stopped short. He'd been lifting his eyes towards the hallway as he was talking to her, and he was blessed with the sight of Jenny standing in the doorway, naked and dripping wet. Jenny always drip-dried, and she had done so ever since he had known her. He never had gotten a coherent reason for this, though he'd asked plenty of times. It was as if she was possessed with a phobia of towels. And even though he'd seen her nude upwards of a million times now, he still ogled her as if he were a teenager seeing a girl naked for the first time, a stupid, open-mouthed grin splitting his face. The only thing missing was the drool.

Not that he minded at all.

Jenny was a thin woman, thirty-one years old. She had dark brown hair, which now looked black from the moisture, and beautiful brown eyes a man could happily get lost within. She was roughly five-feet, three-inches and was an absolute knockout in every way. She was soft where she should be, toned where she shouldn't be, and she curved in all the right places, at just the right angles.

She smiled at him as he gawked, his mouth still hanging open stupidly. The vacant drool was now beginning to collect in the corner of his mouth.

"You were saying, dear?" Jenny chimed in finally, a hint of a chuckle on her voice.

John's head snapped up and he managed to close his loose jaw as he wiped the corner of his mouth with his hand. The drool *had* made an appearance, the tardy bastard. He looked her in the eye for the first time since coming home. It took a moment to compose himself, squirming and making adjustments to his jeans, which were now suspiciously too tight around the groin.

"I, uh, I was asking if you got in touch with, um, La-Larry today?" he said, finally.

He couldn't form a fucking sentence. He *knew* she knew her exposure did this to him. It always had. With any other woman he'd ever known, he'd been cool, relaxed. He was mister Suave himself. But not with Jenny, not a bit, and she fucking well knew it. He could see it in her eyes too, the little gleam, the *sparkle* which told him so. She turned him into a bumbling high-schooler about to split his damn jeans open with his rod and flood the room from his aching balls, and she was relishing it! His loins ached for her. Something had to give, and it had better give soon.

"No," she said, shaking her head, small beads of water tinkling to her shoulders as she did. "I tried calling him several times today and kept getting the fucking machine. I guess he's out."

John could hardly hear what she was saying. His eyes were following the little beads of water on her shoulders, which were now trailing over the swell of her perfect breasts, then racing for the beautiful, bald triangle between her legs.

He shook his head and wrenched his eyes back to hers.

"W-what, I'm sorry?" he stuttered.

She smiled and repeated herself.

Concern now overtook him as he clearly heard her words. Larry was supposed to have called them as soon as he was at his place in Greenville, about halfway between Winnsboro and Dallas. That had been two days ago. They should've heard from him by now, and things were getting tense with Tony.

This wasn't like Larry. Not at all.

"Did Jimmy ever call?" he asked, finally focusing on something other than her body.

"Yeah," Jenny said, a hint of concern in her own eyes now. "He called last night. About eleven, or so. Said things were good on his end, but, Johnny, I..."

She trailed off and John's eyes narrowed.

"What?"

She shrugged. "I dunno, maybe it's nothing. It's just, the way he was talking. It reminded me of when, well...you know."

John did know, and a knot began to form in his stomach.

"Fuck," was all he could manage.

He started to sigh when her eyes brightened a shade and she asked, "What about you? Where have you been?" She was an expert at changing the subject. John was thankful.

The question carried a bit of a *how-dare-you-stay-out-all-night-without-calling-me* tone with it, and a look to match. He supposed he deserved it. It wasn't like him to do so, not without calling her, anyway. But he'd had his reasons last night. He'd been out late, near Dallas, working out a deal to surprise the love of his life. Then he'd had too much to drink and crashed in a motel. He didn't need to get a DWI with the two duffel bags in the trunk. They would raise questions he couldn't answer.

But, in spite of her mild scolding, Jenny's personality was as perfect as her body. She was no nag, and she didn't punish him when he did stupid things. She really was perfect.

He smiled at her in his most charming way, flashing his not-quite-pearly whites.

"You're gonna love me."

She smiled back at him, stepped toward him still dripping.

"Baby, I already love you," she said, a seductive huskiness in her voice now. "You know that."

"Yeah, but I mean you're really gonna love me," His grin turned mischievous, and he paused to add some suspense to the moment.

"What the hell, Johnny?"

"You know what we've been talking about doing but haven't done yet because we didn't wanna bring any attention to ourselves too quickly? What we've been waiting to do now for about ten months?"

Her face seemed to drain of its color as her eyes doubled in size.

"YOU DIDN'T!" she almost cried, both hands clasping over her mouth, her breasts squashed together beneath her arms. "Shut up! You're lying to me! You're a fucking liar! No way, did you really get it?"

She almost screamed with delight as she shoved him in the chest with both arms, enough to knock him off balance.

He smiled, catching himself on the dresser and nearly knocking his empty beer bottle on the floor.

"Come here," he said, then nodded toward the bedroom window.

She ran across the room and threw the shades open, oblivious now to her nudity, and saw it. It sat in one of their two assigned parking spots in the complex, sparkling in the light, a metallic sheen with dancing prisms bouncing off it at every angle.

It was a brand-new Subaru WRX. Four doors, turbos, low to the ground, all-wheel-drive, and nightmare fast. They had wanted one ever since John had pulled his last job, but they had been laying low for a while. On paper, they just didn't make a lot of money, but of course what they really made wasn't on paper anywhere. Nowhere the government looked, anyway. Jumping into a purchase like this after the last job would have sent red flags up all over the place, and they couldn't afford for that to happen. They had put some of the money from the last job into their account in the beginning—not much, just a couple thousand dollars— and added to it incrementally over the past months to keep things looking Kosher on paper. And with the heat now pretty well diminished, John had decided to pick up the car for his girl.

"OH, I LOVE YOU! I love you! I love you! I love you!" she repeated over and over, never looking away from the car.

As John smiled broadly, he swung his gaze away from his

beautiful, naked love, and caught site of a young boy of no more than thirteen. He was riding his bike by the car, and John watched the boy stop to look at it. His young eyes were wide and fascinated, looking over the car with something which may have bordered on lust. Jenny squealed again, her joy overcoming her, and the boy's head snapped up, alarm in his eyes. Within about a half-second, his eyes widened and became more round, but the longing quality in them never changed. It seemed that his lust had shifted objects, and he had decided he would rather look at Jenny than the car. Especially in her current attire.

"Is that sweet or what?" John asked.

"Oh, it's perfect!" Jenny chirped, thinking he was speaking of the car, and kissed him. "I love it!"

"No, I mean—"

She turned back to the window and John saw her notice the young boy looking at her, and he stopped trying to explain. Never one to succumb to embarrassment, Jenny smiled at the boy, blew him a kiss, and turned back into the room out of his view. John stifled a laugh and watched terror steal over the young boy's face, and an instant later he was peddling away as fast as he could, standing on the pedals, the bike swaying back and forth over the pavement. A block or so down the street, the boy literally leaped off his bike, leaving it to crash unceremoniously to the grass of a yard, and the sprinting boy disappeared up the steps to another condo and inside. He clearly had urgent business to attend to.

"Fap away, little man," John chuckled as he drew the blinds.

He turned back to Jenny, the urgency in his loins returning. But Jenny wasn't smiling anymore, despite her outburst a moment ago over the car and her clear delight in John having purchased it, she now seemed curious and almost apprehensive.

"What is it?" John asked, his brow furrowing.

She feigned a smile which quickly retreated.

"Are you sure it's all over with? You sure we ain't gonna get any trouble from Big Brother over this? You talked to Tony before you did this, right? We don't need any heat over this. You know what they...what they might find."

"I'm positive," John said, smiling and waving his hands

dismissively. "I talked to the motherfucker. We're all clear."

The 'motherfucker' was Tony, a part of their crew. No one in the crew was happy to have a dirty cop on board, but it was what it was. No changing it, not now. Not after the night John had gone searching for Jimmy and—

"But how?" she asked, her arms folding beneath the swell of her bosom and pulling John's spiteful thoughts of Tony away.

"You remember the marked bills we separated?" John asked.

She nodded.

"Well, they turned up," he went on. "Tony said the department grabbed up some half-retarded kid with some of the bills Jimmy and I separated from the score. We just put them on the street, pretty anonymously. No one knew where they came from. The dude came across them and—like any dumb hick—snatched them up. I mean, we were hoping for something like this, but it couldn't have worked out any better. Fucking guy is too damned stupid to even come up with a story. Like I said, half a retard, but it worked out for us. Cops locked him up and he's going away for it. They're asking for names, of course. They can see how stupid he is, no way he pulled it off alone, but it's like he's just shut down. Almost catatonic." He shrugged. "So they're going to let him take the fall for it. A town like this doesn't have the money, manpower, or will to make much more of it. At this point, they're just thankful to save a little face."

"I guess so," she started, though John could see in her eyes she was not thrilled about some poor, innocent, and stupid kid going away for what he and the others had done. Still, she didn't seem to be so torn up about it to give it more than an initial thought.

"What about the rest of the money?" she asked, seeming to dismiss her conscience. "Aren't they gonna want to find it?"

"Of course," John said, shrugging, "but they think this guy grabbed a little spending cash and sent off the rest to be laundered somewhere." John laughed, shaking his head. "And the fucking retard is still too stupid to say otherwise! This couldn't have turned out better!"

A shred of her conscience gleamed back in her eyes.

"Don't say that, Johnny," she said quietly, looking to the floor.

He looked at her a moment, his smile faltering.

"Say wha—"

"You know what I mean," she said, cutting him off curtly. "We've done a lot of bad shit in our lives, but I don't need Karma crawling up our ass for laughing at re...folks less fortunate."

"Okay, okay," John said, his hands up in mock surrender, "I apologize. Anyway..."

He trailed off a moment, trying to think of how to change the subject. He didn't share her talent for such, but he found something and went on.

"Larry got me set up with the documents a few days ago when I picked the bags up from him. Standard shit, I inherited some money from a dead uncle and all that. It'll pass muster, especially around here. He promised. So, at least with this one, we are one hundred percent in the clear. He's gonna do something similar for this score we pulled a couple of days ago, too, just with Jimmy this time. You can only have so many dead uncles, you know?"

"You have the bags here?" she asked apprehensively.

"It's fine, babe," he said, crossing to her and stroking her arms in his hands. "Martha Savage didn't raise no fool."

He grinned at her, looking over her body again, longingly.

"Babe, you sure know how to wear that," he said, his eyes full of desire.

When his eyes returned to hers, she was smiling back at him, a mischievous grin twisting up from one corner of her mouth. Her resignations were fading. He could always do that for her. Put her at ease. Make her feel safe. He supposed it was why she'd chosen him from the beginning, and why she'd stayed all these years.

She pressed her body into his. Slowly.

"So, you wanna give it a spin?" he asked, a strange croak in his voice as he felt her warmth. Her arms swung listlessly at her sides now, her hair still dripping, her body seeming to sparkle as light danced in the beads of water all over her.

"You bet I want to..." she said gazing up into his eyes. Her lips were close to his.

She kissed him then, and he could feel the firmness of her nipples pushing against his chest. All thoughts of Subarus, Larry and Tony and Jimmy, the dumb hick, all gone now. And he was glad to be rid of them.

She rubbed her hand against his firm groin, seeming to ache through his jeans. He shuddered.

"Good thing I know how to drive a stick."

John grinned, knowing he looked precisely like the boy on his bike a few moments before.

"You know, I always say—"

"Shut the fuck up, Johnny."

She smiled and threw him down on the bed. Then they did what came naturally.

# Chapter 3

About two hours later, they came down the stairs, relaxed and fulfilled. They decided to take the car for a spin. It was everything they had expected and more. Acceleration like a sprinting demon, all the amenities inside. Bluetooth, satellite radio, power windows and locks. It even had a six-speed manual transmission, which, as Jenny had proclaimed earlier in their bedroom, she was proficient with.

They laughed as they drove, holding hands when they could afford a single hand on the wheel. They even pulled off on a country road outside of town, an old gravel road off Mitchell Street which looked to have been little more than a forgotten trail, and they made love again, properly Christening their new vehicle.

After some time, they finally returned. They made their way into the condo. Jenny kissed him, then went upstairs. John smiled as he watched her ascend the stairs, only turning away once she was out of sight. He pulled out his cell phone and dialed a number.

"Hello?" a voice on the other answered. It sounded annoyed. Agitated. Maybe even just the slightest bit slurred.

"Jimmy?" John replied, concerned. "It's John. What's happening? Any word from Larry yet?"

"Oh, hey Johnny," Jimmy said. "What's up?"

A crunching noise through the receiver. Jimmy was chewing on something.

"That's what I'm asking you, bud," John replied.

Something was off. Something was *way* off. What had Jenny said earlier about Jimmy?

*It reminded me of when, well...you know.*

"Right," Jimmy came on again, his voice tapering off.

*Is he high again?* John thought to himself. *I thought he'd kicked that shit.*

"Jimmy, you straight?" John asked, cutting through the bullshit.

There was a short intake of breath on the other end, then Jimmy's voice was back on, mild indignation in its tone.

"The fuck you ask me something like that for, Johnny?"

No denial. Not even misdirection. Just the response of a petulant child, angry for being called out.

"You know why, Jimmy. I need to know. We *have* to be straight right now."

Silence. There was no sound on the line aside from the occasional exhale of air.

"Jimmy, god-dammit, are you on that shit again?" John barked into the phone.

"Fuck you, Johnny! No! Alright? I'm not on that shit! Jesus Christ, what an asshole! You're not my moth—"

"Yeah, yeah, and I ain't your fucking priest neither, but I can't have you running around on that shit. Not again. So excuse me if I don't give a fuck about your feelings on the matter."

He stopped, wincing inwardly at himself for being so harsh, but not apologizing for it. He squinted his eyes and rubbed the bridge of his nose, taking in a few deep breaths before going on.

"Listen, that's not why I called," John finally said, sighing heavily. "Have you heard from Larry yet?"

"No. No I ain't," Jimmy said after a pause, the indignation in his tone fading now. "Like I told you before, I thought he was supposed to be in touch as soon as he got out of the city and got to his place in

Greenville, but I never heard from him. That's all I know."

There was a waver in Jimmy's voice at the end, and it was so genuine that John believed him. Larry had done a lot for Jimmy. Hell, so had John himself, but with Larry it was different. Jimmy had come to see the man as a sort of father-figure. Even though they were only separated by ten years in age, the chasm between them in mental maturity was a near immeasurable canyon.

If Jimmy knew what was up with Larry, he would talk.

"Well, nobody's heard from him since he left Dallas and I'm starting to get a little worried. He's supposed to take this stuff and have it looked at."

John was now talking in code. 'Stuff' meant 'cash' and 'having it looked at' was to have it 'laundered'. They never spoke of their business dealings over the phone, not openly anyway, not unless it was in code.

"Well," Jimmy started, "I know a guy who could do a little looking into for us, but I'm not so sure he's on the level. I mean, he's a good dude but—"

"Then he's not a god-damn option, Jimmy!" John snapped, cutting him off. "Do you think? Do you *ever* think? Christ, sometimes the people you know scare the shit out of me."

"I'm sorry, Johnny," Jimmy said, sounding a little wounded. "Cool down. I ain't never used the guy, I just said I know him, is all. Just putting it out there. I mean, fuck, man."

"Well, quit putting that shit out there. It's useless and god-damned careless."

John was thoroughly upset now.

"Okay, okay," Jimmy said, the wounded tone in his voice resurfacing. "Geez, I'm sorry."

John took a long, steadying breath. He was overreacting. He knew it. The idea of Jimmy being back on the shit had sent John into a tantrum. An understandable tantrum, but a tantrum all the same. He could see in his mind's eye Jimmy lying there on that mattress on the floor, the needle hanging from a festering sore in his arm, mouth lolled open.

And, of course, there was the dirty guy digging through his pockets.

Ah, yes, how could he forget the dirty man? The news later identified him as "Lucky" Lou Garber, which John had found ironic. He had been lucky, alright. Just not in the good sense. Everything from that moment had overtaken John in the worst kind of way, and he hadn't even realized what he'd done until it was too late.

The smoking gun in John's hand.

The man lying on the floor, holding his bleeding gut.

The filthy lips trying to form words, but only producing black, slimy blood which dripped from his mouth in dark strings.

John pushed the memories away, a chill receding down his back now. He exhaled.

"No, I'm sorry," he said. "I'm just on edge with all this stuff here and no way to move it yet. And to top it all off I can't find Larry and that's got me shitting bricks. You think he got picked up?"

"No way," Jimmy said assuredly. "No one even knew the shit was gone. Even *now* no one knows. Ain't been on the news or nothing. Kind of weird, actually. Whose place was that anyway?"

"No idea," said John. "Ask the motherfucker who set it up."

John paused a moment, sighing out his frustration and considering.

"Say," he said after several seconds, "you think you can swing up Greenville way and peek in on Larry? I'm sure everything's fine, but it won't hurt to check, anyway. And he'll probably be glad to see you."

Jimmy said nothing for a few moments, but John could hear the air catch in his throat. He was hesitating. For what reason, John had no clue, but he was sure Jimmy was hesitating.

*Because he's fucking high, that's why! He doesn't want Larry of all people to see him like that again!*

While John wanted to dismiss this thought, he couldn't. He couldn't think of a single other reason why Jimmy wouldn't be willing to go and check on Larry right away. The very fact he hadn't already volunteered to do so was telling.

"Jimmy?" John finally asked the silence. "Jimmy, you still

there?"

There was a cough, another sound like crunching candy, then, "Yeah, sorry. I'm here."

"Well, what do you think? Can you swing out there or what?"

John was becoming increasingly agitated.

*He's high as a kite!*

"Sure," Jimmy finally answered in a wavering voice. "Sure, yeah, I'll go check on him."

John nodded to the empty room. "Good. You call me when you know something. And Jimmy..."

A few beats passed before Jimmy answered.

"What is it?"

"Stay straight. I mean it."

There was an exasperated sigh on the other end, but John thought it sounded a little forced.

"Yeah, Johnny, I got it. Jesus fu—"

John hung up.

His worry about Larry was building to a fever-pitch. The more he thought of it, the worse it got. The money was here, right in his goddamned living room, and Larry was the man to move it. But no one knew where Larry was.

Jimmy had him worried too, but he wasn't going to waste time listening to Jimmy's bullshit retorts bemoaning John's unreasonable assumptions about him being back on the shit. John knew better, and Jimmy should too.

*What a fuck up.*

Larry had always worked with John, Jimmy, and Tony on their various jobs. But Larry Horowitz wasn't a get-your-hands-dirty kind of guy. He was an information guy, a strategic guy, a logistics guy. He heard things in his profession, serving society's unsavory and unpalatable, and he knew when something seemed like a decent score and when it didn't. If something sounded good, minimal risk, he checked it out. If he liked what he saw, he called John and they went from there.

He was also good at procuring the tools necessary to follow through on their work. Once, when he'd realized they were going to need to actually blow the hinges off a safe, he'd managed to come up with a small amount of malleable plastic explosive, replete with wires and detonating rods, along with thorough instructions on exactly how to utilize such equipment without blowing your own balls off, never mind your hands.

"Where the hell did you find this shit?" John had asked him, marveling over the explosive.

Larry had laughed, clapped him on the shoulder, and winked.

"Don't ask, don't tell."

John and Jimmy—and in the past couple of years, Tony as well—would do the actual work. Larry took his cut on the back end, often at a higher share than the others, and that was mostly fine with everyone. Mostly, because on more than one occasion, Tony had taken issue with it. But only privately, and he quickly dismissed the subject. Larry was just too valuable, and they all knew it. Not only did he find them work, he made the work possible, and was able to clean up the payout. Didn't matter how much money you scored, if it was marked or traceable, it was no good. But Larry could fix that.

So, yeah, Larry was valuable. *Very* damned valuable. If they were working, it was because Larry had set the job up.

At least, that was, until this last time.

# Chapter 4

Tony had come up with a plan.

He had called them all over to his house. This was highly irregular—it was no secret that there was little love lost between Tony and the others—but he'd talked them into it with promises of beer and barbecue. They met at his place one evening, and the motherfucker had bullshitted his way across any number of subjects—most of them pedestals on which he would prop himself in expectation of their groveling worship—laughing at all his own jokes as he went. The others obliged with polite smiles.

"So, I got the guy pulled over, short little shit, and I can tell he's shaking in his britches. He gives me his ID and insurance card, and I ask him what he's so freaked out about. Guy says, 'nothing, I just don't want no ticket.' But he's got this hot piece of ass in the passenger seat, and right away I can tell she's way out of his league. So I figure escort, right? Anyway, I could've nailed him to the wall on it, but all these cunts running around the streets here think they don't gotta play by the rules like everybody else. Think they're above the law."

He had paused, laughing and shaking his head, taking another pull on his beer.

"So anyway," Tony went on with his tiresome story, "I call the little fucker out on it. Right away he's freaking out, and the bitch actually leans over him, I mean takes charge right away, got her tits all dangling in front of me. And the look on the little guy's face makes me think he's blowing his load right then and there, what with her jugs bouncing next to his face. So she asks me if something can be done about this. Could we work something out? I figure a guy can't never get too many BJs in his life, so I tell her it's that or I break out the bracelets."

He beamed proudly at this, looking around at the other three, red-faced with laughter at his story.

He went on.

"So, they follow me around to the park—it's deserted that time of night—and she gargles my swimmers right in front of the guy. And she was a pro, alright, let me tell you. She's had *lots* of practice. Anyway, the little fucker in the car never took his eyes off us the whole time, the pervert. So anyhow, I let them go, but not before making the bitch give the guy a big kiss, tongue and all. I pulled up next to them right after, rolled down my window, and tell the guy, 'Pretty sweet, ain't it?'"

Fresh guffaws erupted from Tony at this, and he seemed oblivious to the disgust of the other three. John had no delusions of their morality, but he couldn't fathom the depravity of Officer Tony Tribbiani. The man made his stomach turn.

"Yeah, they're all cunts out there," Tony said after his laughter died down and took another swig of beer. "All of them. Running around in their Volvos and their Tahoes and their fucking Mercedes. Think they're fancy with their shiny new iPhones and god-damn lap dogs. Fucking cunts."

He stopped for a while, drinking his beer, and the silence dragged on long enough that John finally broke in on the conversation.

"What's this got to do with anything, Tony?"

Tony's face turned serious, and his eyes narrowed as he leaned forward and looked all three of them in the face. It was a ridiculous look, but none of them laughed. They all knew what kind of man he was, and a man like that with a badge to boot was the most dangerous kind.

"Point of the story, Savage," he said in a low, even tone, "is there are things in the world worth having, and having a lot of."

"Like pussy?" Jimmy cut in, and laughed himself, but Tony's steely gaze cut it off.

"Not pussy, junkie. Power is what I'm talking about. Power makes the world go 'round. It gets things done."

Larry had leaned in then, spreading his hands and adopting his best courtroom demeanor.

"Okay, sure, but what does that have to do with—"

"A badge carries a lot of power," Tony said, cutting Larry off as if he'd never spoken. "That's how come I could get big tits the other night to swallow my spunk. But there's something else that carries even more power than that, if you've got enough of it, that is."

John and the others had just stared at him.

"Money, you cunts!" he bellowed, suddenly becoming furious and red-faced, his fist slamming the table and causing all their beer bottles to jump and rattle. "Christ, what the hell you think I'm talking about?"

John leaned forward again, his hands up in a calming gesture.

"Okay, okay, we hear you. But you're already in with us. Hell, you make a full salary *plus* what we take on jobs. We're not getting rich, but greedy people get caught—"

"They only get caught when they're stupid," Tony growled. "And I ain't stupid. Larry here ain't stupid, neither. Jury's still out on you and junkie-boy over here."

Jimmy's face had grown scarlet and he'd opened his mouth to say something when Larry had put a hand on his shoulder to stop him.

John glared at Tony, angry with himself for letting him talk him into coming to this bullshit dinner, and huffed a sigh.

"I'm done with this shit," John said and started to stand up.

"Sit down, killer," Tony said, his hand gesturing him back into his seat. "Don't forget how you got your nickname."

John's face flushed so hot he thought it might melt the skin right off him, but he sat down, the curses flying in his mind capable of embarrassing Satan himself.

"I get worked up sometimes when I've had a couple beers too many," Tony said, shrugging and then opening another one. "Forgive me."

He took three long gulps and placed the bottle down in front of him.

"Okay, so what are you saying, Tony?" Larry asked, diplomacy dripping from his tone. "You want a bigger cut? Is that the deal?"

Tony paused, the bottle nearly to his lips for another pull, then he put it back down with an icy stare.

"No," he said. "That ain't what I'm saying. I'll cut to the chase."

"That'd be nice," John blurted before he could get his hands on the words and wrestle them back down his throat. He winced, expecting another verbal barrage.

Instead, Tony just looked at him a moment, then back to Larry, and went on.

"I know a guy. Works for Dallas PD. Went to the Academy together, we go way back. Anyway, there's a nut-job going up for manslaughter, something about a barfight gone bad. Doesn't matter. What matters is he's going up, but he's got a safe full of cash just sitting there in his house. Family owns the place, so it's not going back to the bank or anything, but no one's living there right now. It's perfect. And there's supposed to be a lot in there."

Tony was smiling now, his eyes meeting all of theirs in turn. He sounded proud of himself, and the look on his face stated the same.

But as Larry leaned in, Tony's smile began to falter.

"Tony, how would the police know of something like this and not have confiscated it?" he asked, his lawyerly tone in full effect now. "I mean, manslaughter is one thing, but how on earth would they know about a large amount of money and not at least report it to the IRS? I've been a lawyer for a long time, and I'm telling you, that's just not how this works."

Tony's glare was indignant.

"The fuck you saying, Horowitz?"

"What I want to know is what aren't you telling us?"

Larry's hands were outstretched on either side, a confounded look of wonder on his face. John was liking this. The idea of the money had almost got his dick hard at first, but seeing Larry make Tony's story look like something a kindergartner would conjure up was much better. He put his hand over his mouth to hide a smile.

Tony continued to glare for a moment, then in an instant his glare vanished and he smiled.

"Well," he said, shifting gears, "that's where my buddy comes in. He talked to the guy on the way to the station. He was the one who picked him up. When the guy mentioned the money, you know, his mic and all *malfunctioned* and he heard the guy out. The guy thought he could buy off my pal, get him to let him go, I guess. But that wasn't happening. Instead, we've got gold sitting two hours from here, just waiting for us to go pick it up."

Both Larry and John's eyes were narrowed, trying to gauge the story Tony had just told them. Jimmy's, on the other hand, were wide with excitement.

"Shit!" Jimmy said. "Fucking-A, I'm in!"

Larry and John had looked at Jimmy, uncertainty on their faces, then John turned back to Tony.

"How much?" he asked.

Tony's smile broadened. "How's six hundred K sound?"

There were audible gasps from all three of the others. They had never taken anything *close* to that before. And John hadn't realized until it was all over how much it had clouded his vision.

"There's just one catch," Tony said after they'd all had time to absorb the information. "Not really a catch, just a few nuances we have to work out."

"This isn't how we do things," Larry said in a whisper, staring at the empty bottle of beer in front of him. "We have a process—"

But John had grabbed his arm under the table and Larry hadn't said another word of protest.

"Me and my pal with DPD will have to run some security," Tony continued. "So I can't be there. We'll be around, but I can't be in the house. Larry can go in my stead."

Larry's face looked stunned, but John had squeezed his arm

tighter and Larry had kept quiet.

There was silence in the room as Tony looked around at them all, and it was Jimmy who broke it finally.

"Well, I don't know about y'all, but I'm fucking in!"

John had found he was nodding, almost unperceptively at first, but nodding just the same. He allowed it to continue and intensify until he too was throwing his hat in the ring. Larry was last, and most reluctant—he hadn't ever gone on a single job in the flesh—but he finally agreed. Lawyers were always seeing dollar signs, John figured, and it had won him over.

"Good," Tony said, and cracked another beer. He handed out three more to the others. "So, we're doing it. I'll talk to my boy and let you know when, but it'll be soon. Can't let a thing like that sit there too long."

They drank their beers, and the conversation had turned to more casual things, and another story of Tony's debauchery with the Winnsboro PD. But John had tuned him out. He was thinking of the money, sitting in Dallas, waiting for him to come and get it.

*Six hundred thousand dollars,* he thought, and smiled.

"Alright, you cunts!" Tony had said, stepping out his back door and opening his grill, which billowed smoke. "Let's fucking eat!"

# Chapter 5

Tony's pal with DPD managed to get the alarm codes. Apparently, it wasn't hard to do when you had a badge and didn't mind putting it to use. Larry, unable to separate himself from the lawyer inside of him—though dubiously capable of dismissing any moral outrage at his own criminal endeavors—had inquired how such a dismissal of the Fourth Amendment was possible.

"What the hell does it matter, Horowitz?" Tony had asked, a look of stupefied wonder on his face.

"We have a Constitution, for Christ's sake!" Larry had nearly bellowed. "Without a warrant, this kind of thing is—"

"Larry," Tony said, his hand in the air to shut him up. "What exactly do you think we're doing here, huh? You think we're conducting an investigation into tax fraud? We're stealing money. So please, dispose with the Constitutional hero shit."

Larry had set his jaw and popped his neck. John could see he was stung, but the motherfucker was right.

The man going down for manslaughter in a bar fight had a house none of them would have believed. It was no mansion, but it *was* a rather nice suburban home. John estimated it to be well upwards of two-thousand square feet, and was nicely modernized. Not the kind of place you expect someone with such poor decision-making skills to live. But, then again, people tend to not make the best decisions when they're tanked, John reckoned, so he dismissed the line of thought outright.

They'd gone in late. It was well after 1:00 A.M., and the sleepy suburban street was quiet and still. There were street lamps on every fifty yards or so, but luck was with them. The house they were going in to was almost directly in between two of them, and it was as dark a place as the street offered.

The codes worked, even though Larry fumbled it the first time with trembling hands. He really shouldn't have been there, John had thought. But Tony and the DPD guy were out patrolling the surrounding streets, making sure things were secure.

The second try, while red numbers counted down menacingly, letting them know that within the next twenty seconds alarms would be blaring, strobing lights would be lit, and police departments alerted, Larry punched the code in and all the menace stopped. A green-lit display informed them the alarm was DEACTIVATED, and they all let out a wavering sigh of relief.

The safe was in a study off the back end of the rear hallway. There was a fine oak desk with a Macintosh computer sitting to one corner, a few bookshelves behind it, and a large triptych of artwork featuring Bosch's *The Garden of Earthly Delights*. The safe was behind the center piece, built into the wall, and Jimmy went to work on it with his drill.

It took some time, but they finally made it through, and with the help of a thin snake camera, Jimmy found his way to unlocking it.

It was all there, just as Tony had said. Six-hundred-K. Clean, fresh stacks, still with paper wrappings around them indicating ten-thousand dollars per. Their eyes lit up like kids in a candy store, and they started shoveling the money into bags.

When they'd finished, Larry had said, "This stuff is clean."

"What?" Jimmy had asked, his brow furrowed.

"It's clean," Larry said again. "I mean, this isn't something from insurance companies or banks where they mark it or keep sequential serial numbers. Look here."

He flipped out one of the stacks like fanning a deck of cards. He did it slowly, and John and Jimmy saw right away the serial numbers on the bills were completely random.

"What about marks?" John asked. "How can we know they're not mar—"

"Because," Larry said, his eyes bright, "look where we are. Someone with this kind of cash in a personal safe, this is some sort of personal stash fund. Like if you need a lot of money real quick, going to the bank would raise eyebrows. Whoever this guy is, he's been putting it away, a little at a time, for quite a while. If this were a company or a bank, I'd never say this. But..."

He spread his arms around the room. John took the meaning, and Jimmy caught on a moment later. It was clean, alright, and there would be no need to launder it.

"But," Larry said a few moments later, his hand on his chin in thought, "then again, someone so meticulous, putting away like this over time, may have their own system of tracking them. It would still be safer to clean it, even though it's clean already."

John nodded, but he wasn't convinced. No private individual was capable of tracking such things, were they? Didn't that require government resources and technology, only acquirable through court orders? He thought so, but Larry was the attorney, and he deferred to his judgement.

They got out of there without incident, went back to a parking lot of Tom Thumb, where John's car was. They loaded the bags into his trunk and said their goodbyes.

"I've got some business here in town for the next couple of days," Larry said. "I'll be in touch when I get back home. Keep that safe." He pointed to the trunk of John's car.

John winked and made a mock salute, then was gone. He caught a motel, and the next day bought the new car, after much wheeling and dealing. Then he'd gotten drunk and forgotten to call Jenny.

## Chapter 6

Tony never returned John's phone call, but he *did* show up at his apartment within an hour of John trying to reach him.

John noticed him through the window, shuffling up the walkway with his carefree swagger, sunglasses hung neatly over his eyes, his olive skin almost bronze in the sunlight. He wore a pair of jeans and button-down shirt—untucked—and his dark hair was buzzed short into a crew-cut which would have looked utterly ridiculous on anyone else...yet he managed to pull it off.

After three quick knocks, Tony threw open the door and let himself in. John was halfway up from his chair, a frowning, pissed-off quality adorning his face. Tony's arrogance crawled under his skin. He wasn't sure if it was simply poor etiquette from whatever Neanderthal raised Tony or the fact he was a cop—a dirty fucking cop—but the air around him could turn toxic in an instant when he started throwing his balls around a room.

John went ahead and stood all the way, sighing as he did so.

"Hey-hey, my man!" Tony started, pulling his sunglasses off, lips peeling back over his grinning teeth. "What's happening?"

John opened his mouth to say something, but Tony was already looking at the bags on the floor.

"That it?" Tony asked, gesturing to the duffel bags with his glasses.

John nodded. "Yeah, that's it. Listen, have you heard from Larry? And where the hell have you been? I've been trying to call you."

The aggression in his voice was more palpable than he'd intended, but he didn't back off from it.

"Yo, man, I've been a little busy—"

"The fuck you have!" John snapped. "I've been calling. You see a call from me, you answer. Period. We've got too much at stake here to—"

"I don't know who you think you are, Savage, but you can eat my ass," Tony said, his eyes squinting as though to pierce John's skin. "We work *together,* I don't fucking work for you, you get that, motherfucker?"

Tony had crossed the room while speaking, and now the hand holding the glasses was pointing them at John's face like an accusing finger. The irony of the motherfucker calling *him* the motherfucker was not lost on John.

"In case you forgot," Tony went on, "*I'm* the one who set this deal up. You don't have a cut at all if not for me. *And* I'm the one who made sure there was no trouble. I put my damn career on the line for this shit, and you think you're gonna to talk to me like this? You've got another thing coming, asshole!"

John's lips tightened into a thin line and he looked away. This was exactly what pissed him off about Tony. His small-town cop attitude. The big fish in the small pond, demanding everyone worship his swinging dick.

"Where's Larry?" John asked, still not making eye contact with Tony.

Tony held his stance a moment longer, pointing his glasses in John's face, then slackened and backed off a step.

"I have no idea," he said with a shrug.

Now John looked him in the eyes. "No one does. That's the problem. Jimmy's swinging out—"

"Aw, shit, you're sending the junkie out there?" Tony said, a look of disgust on his face.

John took a breath to steady himself and push down the anger of being cut off when speaking.

"Yes," he said through clenched teeth. "He's going up to Greenville to see what's going on. See if Larry's around. This doesn't concern you?"

Tony shrugged, a smug look on his face as he dropped a stem of his glasses over the collar of his shirt.

"Doesn't make a shit to me," Tony said. "Larry's a grown-ass man, he can do what he likes. He doesn't answer to me, I don't answer to him."

John looked away, astonished. Tony and Larry weren't exactly friends, but they'd worked together for years. Hell, they all had. They'd had to trust each other completely, even if they didn't exactly all like each other. That was just part of it. If you couldn't trust the crew you were working with, you shouldn't be doing the job. That's how people got caught.

That's how people got killed.

John's mind was elsewhere, drifting. He was worried about Larry's disappearance, Tony's indifference, and Jimmy's obvious leap from the wagon. They still needed to put the money in a safe place.

He snapped back to the room when he saw Tony picking up the bags with a grunt and throwing them over his shoulders.

"What the hell are you doing?" John asked, taking a step toward the dirty cop who was his partner.

"The hell's it look like I'm doing?" Tony responded, gesturing to the bags with his chin. "I told you we've got to clean this shit, and I've got a guy to do it. I'm taking it over to him. What's the problem?"

"The problem is you," John said shaking his head, a cold look in his eyes. "Something's wrong. You know it, I know it. Even god-damn Jimmy knows it. Thing is, you don't seem to give a shit. It's no secret we aren't friends, but we *are* partners. We look out for each other. Larry is one of us. And *Larry* gets the money cleaned, not that it needs it. But that's beside the point. This is how we do things."

"Oh, sorry," Tony quipped whimsically, rolling his eyes. "I'm supposed to freak out when a grown man doesn't answer his phone? Please. And I don't give a shit how we do things. This is *my* show, and

I'm calling the god-damn shots."

He turned for the door.

"Wait a minute," John said, taking a few steps towards Tony, who was now turning back to face him. "I'll come with you. If we're gonna do it this way, I want to meet your guy. That's a lot of green to be carrying around all by yourself."

"No, no," Tony said, holding up a hand. "I got it, man. Thanks anyways, though."

The sarcasm was a living thing.

"Fuck you, I'm coming," John barked indignantly as he moved within a couple of feet of Tony.

Tony thrust out the hand he'd been holding up and placed it on John's chest. John stopped and looked down at the hand, amazed at the balls on his partner.

He swatted the hand away.

"Get your hands off me!" John hissed. "That's *our* money, asshole, in case you forgot! I don't give a *fuck* if you think this is your show or not, the money is *ours*."

"And it's *my* contact," Tony retorted. "This isn't a fucking drive-through, Savage! These people aren't exactly open about their business dealings. If I bring you in, they instantly turn nervous. They turn nervous, they walk away. And they might not let us do the same. You know better than that."

John glared at Tony, his mouth quivering, breathing hard. He wanted to clock him. Knock his head into next week and send his ass to follow. But he backed off. He clenched and unclenched his fists as he took two steps back.

"Fine," John said through thin lips. "You keep in touch, though, you hear me? You call me when you do the swap, and I want to know what he charges."

"Ten cents on the dollar," Tony said as he turned to the door and stepped through the threshold. John saw him pull his sunglasses off his collar, flick the stems out, and put them on his face.

"I don't like this, Tony," John said in a low voice, but loud enough for the other man to hear. "This isn't how we do things."

Tony stopped halfway down the walkway and half-turned to him. His sunglasses reflected a harsh beam of light which made John squint.

"Things change," Tony said. "Get with it or don't, doesn't make a shit to me. But quit all this bitching."

Tony turned and began walking away again when he said one final thing.

"You're a cunt, Savage. You ain't doing shit about it."

John grabbed the frame of the door and squeezed until his knuckles turned white.

# Chapter 7

John wasn't terrific with money. He could admit it. Of course, he wasn't terrible with it, either. He knew if he'd had a little more discipline, their bank account would be in much better shape than it was now. The stuff didn't exactly burn a hole in his pocket, but he didn't make the best decisions on spending it, either. It wasn't something he was particularly proud of, but he really didn't have any shame on the subject. He was still young, healthy, and could do plenty of work. And now, with what he'd pulled down with this last job, he and Jenny could vanish into the Caribbean if they wanted, open up a little rental shop on a picture-perfect beach somewhere, and be set for life. You didn't have to be terrific with money down there. It went further. Piece of cake.

*You have to get your god-damned money first,* he thought.

The job they had pulled before this last one had set them up with about $20,000 each, spread evenly—except for Larry—across all four of them. It had been the biggest score they had ever pulled off by far at the time.

*Until this last one.*

John had a thing with spending a good chunk of his money as soon as he got it. Or at least as soon as it was safe to start spending, anyway. He had enough discipline to keep it under lock and key until things had cooled down. But when the time came, he was hood rich as long as the money lasted.

Problem was, the money just never lasted. That's why they pulled so many jobs. John wasn't great with money, but Jimmy was downright *stupid* with money. The rest of the crew were always busy with another job because of them. Not that the rest minded. Money was money, and when it was there for the taking, take it they would.

The four of them—John, Jimmy, Larry, and Tony—had been working together now for about three years. John, Jimmy, and Larry had known each other for some time, but a chance encounter with Tony had brought the cop into the fold. They had just pulled a job a week before, and Jimmy had gone missing. John had called Larry, who had no idea where he was either, and the two of them had set out looking for him. Before long, John had a street hood—someone he knew had gotten high with Jimmy in the past—tracked down, and was shoving his face in a toilet which sported a pair of putrefying turds in its slime-filmed bowl, leftovers some junkie had neglected to flush. Arms had thrashed and fecal debris had been spat from the addict's mouth when John had pulled his face out of the toilet by his hair.

"Ready to talk, asshole?" John had said, trying his best to keep his voice menacing while also suppressing the urge to retch at the stench of old shit.

The junkie had spat another kernel of turd from his lips, vomited, and then nodded his head.

Jimmy was at a house on Pine Street, right at the junction of Main. It was an odd place for such a house: three stories, bedrooms rented out with common areas like bathrooms and kitchen and living areas which were shared by all. At one time it had been a majestic and beautiful home owned by the Mayor of Winnsboro back in the sixties. Now, it was a huge, rotting drug house.

It wasn't even in a bad neighborhood, which added to its oddity. But, in spite of frequent complaints by neighbors and numerous code violations, the house stood on, filled with unsavory types partying and fucking each other on washing machines by windows in full view of neighbors. WPD, it seemed, was more concerned with writing speeding tickets than cleaning up the otherwise decent neighborhood.

Larry had come along, concerned for Jimmy, but when they got to the house, John had gone in alone. Larry stayed in the car, ready to drive them away as soon as John had Jimmy out. Larry was the only one of them who had the appearance of respectability, and he couldn't be found in such a place, even though its inhabitants were precisely the kind of people who had made him wealthy.

John charged in and went room to room looking for Jimmy. In one room where he'd thrown the door open in his search, he found a man who appeared to be nearly fifty years old, but who was more likely closer to his mid-thirties, biting a leather belt in his teeth, the other end looped over his bicep, a hypodermic needle spiked in the crook of his arm.

"Where is he?" John had asked.

"Dude, what?" the junkie had responded, a stupefied glaze in his eyes.

John crossed the room, pulling an old Beretta from his waistband and slapping the man across the face. The needle in his arm fell to the floor with a clatter and a thin stream of blood began to leak from his nose.

John cocked the hammer, the barrel still pointing to the floor.

"Jimmy," John said with a growl. "About my age, dark hair, probably shooting the same shit you are."

The junkie looked to the floor where his needle lay, a droplet of blood hanging precariously from its point. Then he looked back up to John pointing to the ceiling.

"Man, I think maybe he's upstairs, I don't know for sure what room."

John marched up the stairs. His eyes were seared by the sight of a couple balling on a dirty mattress as he passed one room, the door wide open. As he stared for a moment, horrified by the sight but unable to look away, he realized there wasn't a door at all, only a sheet tacked to the frame which they'd neglected to draw across the entryway. Their bodies were emaciated and pock-scarred, the battle wounds of thousands of injections of low-grade trash, and the horrific sounds of their wheezing breath as they huffed with each thrust and the wet slapping of their loins were an offence to his ears. He finally pulled his eyes away from the aberration and moved on down the hall without bothering to draw their curtain.

He finally found Jimmy in the last room on the left. He was passed out on a mattress, the twin of the one the junkie couple down the hall were desecrating.

As John was still taking in the scene of his friend lying there, a belt loose around his arm and a needle still protruding from his skin, John realized they weren't alone in the room. Rage filled him at the sight of Jimmy in such a state, and at such a time as this—they'd just finished a job, for fuck's sake-they couldn't afford to get picked up right then. His hands were trembling, the Beretta still in his right hand tremoring as anger flooded him.

Their visitor was an older man, a scraggly white beard which seemed to have never been graced with a comb, spewed from his face in all directions. Grimy hands tipped with black-crusted nails were reaching into Jimmy's pocket, a black hole which was the man's mouth hung open in an excited *oh*, random black and brown stumps jutting from his gums.

John hadn't been aware he was raising the gun until it went off in his hand. The old man's cheek had exploded, then his forearm as he raised it to fend off whatever was coming at him. Another round had gone into the man's chest and the final one into his belly.

The man slumped over on the mattress next to Jimmy, who was spattered with a misting of the man's blood and still completely passed out.

"Oh, fuck me," John had whispered, a tremor in his voice.

Sounds had erupted as others in the house screamed and scrambled to get out. John crossed the room, slapping Jimmy awake and getting him to his feet, tucking himself under Jimmy's shoulder to get him moving. The old man groaned next to them, holding his bleeding stomach with blood-slick hands. John had ignored his dying whimpers and moved Jimmy towards the door.

They got into the hall, passed the room where the abominable couple were still fucking—they either hadn't heard the shots or were too high and excited to give a damn—and made their way down the stairs.

John managed to get Jimmy into the back of the car and jump

in the passenger seat before they heard the first wails of sirens.

"Drive!" John growled at Larry.

Larry, whose eyes had been as wide as his mouth, dropped the car into gear and stomped the accelerator to speed away.

"What the fuck happened?" he had asked John after they turned on the first street they came to with a squeal of tires.

"I fucked up," John whispered as his shaking hand covered his face. "Oh, Jesus, I fucked up!"

Of course, saying he had 'fucked up' was a phenomenal understatement. John had a mean streak in him. Always had. He was prone to violence from time to time, especially if he'd been drinking, but it had always been of the knuckles and elbows variety. He'd gotten the gun on a whim some years back. He'd done a job on his own and nearly been caught. If it hadn't been for the guard's rotund belly and the mild coronary he'd incurred as he gave chase to the handkerchief-befaced John, he'd likely be in prison now. But the incident had gotten him thinking about things, and he decided it would be a good idea to get a gun, especially in the kinds of circles his line of work often drew him to. Double-crosses were common, and he'd decided he needed something with more bite than his fists to protect himself—and Jenny—with.

But he'd never used it. Not even to scare people with. Not until that night, anyhow. And look what that had gotten him.

John couldn't fathom what had come over him in that moment. He didn't know the old man from Adam, and he was pretty sure the only harm the guy had meant was to lift whatever was left of Jimmy's stash off his person. Yet John had killed the man for it.

*Murdered* him for it.

His mind's eye recalled the blown-apart face and arm, the jets of blood pumping from the man's chest and belly. He felt sick, and for several moments he was certain he was going to lose everything in his guts. But his stomach settled after a few moments, and he leaned his head back against the headrest, beads of sweat cropping on his brow.

But as John tried to wonder why he'd just done such a thing, he realized he already knew deep down. In the depths of his darkening soul lurked a nemesis he'd been running from for years. He'd even eventually attempted to do battle with it a few times. Only that night, three years ago, he'd lost the battle in devastating fashion.

It was fear.

A clawed and fanged monster prowling at the edge of shadows, concealing its beastly face only to heighten the terror within its foe of the greatest fear of them all: the unknown.

John feared his friend—his *brother*—might be dead. When he'd seen Jimmy lying there, his first thought was that he must be dead. And the idea of anyone else touching his dead friend had sent abject terror through his entire system, to the point he'd reacted without being capable of forethought. If he *had* been capable, he'd have never done it. He knew this. He was no killer. No monster. Fear was the monster, and it had asserted its control over him. There was a dead man on that mattress alright. But it wasn't Jimmy. It wasn't John.

And it wasn't the monster.

The fear-beast had won, and John could feel it—almost *hear* it—laughing at him as they sped away. Tears stung his eyes and his throat began to close. A sob almost tore free, but fresh fear grabbed the emotion and strangled it to death in his throat.

It had been Officer Tony Tribbiani who had caught up with them. The knock had come at around 12:15 A.M., startling them all. Larry was still there, Jimmy, still out on the couch, and Jenny had coffee on.

"Who the fuck is that?" Larry had hissed, his normally neat hair askew atop his head.

"I-I..." was all John could say.

He made his way to the window and peaked out. All traces of breath were vacuumed from his pulmonary system in an instant as he saw the uniformed police officer standing on his stoop. A police cruiser was parked at the curb, but there were no lights flashing. The man seemed to be alone as well, though John knew there was always another not far away. If the man wanted backup, he'd have it in no time flat.

John looked back into the room at the others, his eyes wider than he'd remembered them ever being.

"Cops!" he wheezed, his voice low.

Jenny froze, a pot of coffee in her hand, its contents in turmoil as her hand trembled, and Larry's face drained of all color. Jimmy was lying on the couch, stirring a bit, but still mostly out. But the worst part was he was still wearing the clothes from earlier, speckled with the bearded man's blood. Larry pushed back from the kitchen table so fast his chair tumbled over backwards and he raced to throw a blanket over Jimmy. Once this was done, he looked up to John, trying to hide his terror but only having mild success. He nodded.

John let the cop in.

"Got a call about a homicide over on Pine Street earlier this evening," the cop said as he'd come in and John read the nametag on his breast which sported his name. "Seems some neighbors saw a couple of guys jump into the back of a car and speed away right after it happened. Damn fools didn't get any plate numbers, but they had a decent description of the car."

John and the others stood stock still in the living room. Jimmy moaned quietly on the couch but stayed still.

Jenny moved into the room, still holding the coffee pot, and said, "Well, that's just awful, officer. But I can't imagine what you think we might know about it."

She smiled now, by far the coolest of them all, and offered the man coffee. John's throat closed off completely. He didn't want to be having coffee with the police, he wanted to get them out of here as soon as possible. What the fuck was she thinking? Was she out of her mind?

"I'd love a cup, ma'am," the cop said, then winked at John as he strode past him towards the kitchen.

John's breathing had returned, but it took great effort to hold it steady and keep from hyperventilating. The cop passed Jimmy on the couch, whose face was turned away, hiding the speckles of dried blood.

"Rough night for your friend here?" the cop asked.

John and Larry exchanged glances, then Larry took charge.

"He had a few too many, if you know what I mean," he said with a nervous laugh. "Sleeping it off now."

The cop nodded, studying Larry's face for a moment.

"Do I know you?" the cop asked, suspicion on his face.

Larry glanced once more to John, his hands fidgeting nervously over his stomach, then shrugged.

"Uh, perhaps so," he had said. "I-I'm a lawyer. Most of my work is out of Greenville, Rockwall, a little in Dallas. But I've handled a few cases around here in Wood County. Perhaps we've crossed paths there?"

The cop stared at Larry for a long while before smiling. There was real menace in that smile, John remembered, and it had chilled him at that moment.

"Perhaps," the cop said, and took a cup of coffee from Jenny with a nod and a thank you.

"So," he said after taking a sip, "like I said, the neighbors didn't get any plates, but the description of the car was pretty good. Just so happens I saw one that looked pretty close to what they described parked right in front of this condo."

He nodded towards the front door.

"The color was off," he went on, "but that don't mean much. They said black, car out front is more of a dark blue, but hey, it was dark outside, anyway. Easy enough mistake to make."

John felt his bowels loosening. Every muscle in his body was tense now, and he began to sweat even though it was cool in the room.

"I'm sure there's more than one of those cars on the road, officer," Jenny said, smiling and with a chuckle. "They make more than one."

Jimmy stirred on the couch behind the cop and moaned again. The cop looked over his shoulder at him, then back to the John.

"What was he drinking, anyway?"

John barked a nervous laugh that was too loud and too over the top for the situation.

"Oh, you know," he said, then tried to activate his scrambled mind to get it working on a story. "J-just, uh, some vodka. He doesn't use much mixer and—"

"Let me see the bottle," the cop said.

The cop's stare was cold now, penetrating. It bored into John like a diamond flaked drill.

John looked desperately to Jenny, whose cool charade was now crumbling. They had no vodka. There was no vodka bottle in the trash. They had beer, plenty of it, and whiskey too. Why in hell hadn't he said Jimmy had been drinking one of those? Why vodka, for Christ's sake?

"I-I..." John said and trailed off.

The cop's stare continued to bore into him, and John watched as he took another gulp of coffee. He set the cup on the kitchen table and turned back to John, his mouth opening as if to say something, when Jimmy suddenly stood up, throwing off the blanket, and staggering around to face John. He hadn't noticed the cop yet.

"What the fuck happened, Johnny?" Jimmy asked as he pressed his hands to his temples.

The cop was staring at the dark blood stains all over Jimmy's clothes and face. John and Larry froze, Jenny backed against the far wall of the kitchen clutching her chest.

"Well aren't you going to—" Jimmy started and then noticed the cop. "Oh, fuck," he finished.

"Well, well, well," the cop named Tribbiani said. "What's that all over you, boy?"

Jimmy looked down at himself, seeing it for the first time, and became instantly confused. He'd been out before John had ever found him.

"What?" Jimmy said aloud in wonderment, then looked to John. "What happened, man?"

Tony Tribbiani looked back to John with that same menacing smile.

"Looks like I caught myself a killer," he said, his voice almost enthusiastic.

"N-now, just hold on a minute!" John began in protest. "This isn't what it looks like!"

"Oh, no?" Tony said. "Tell me what it's supposed to look like."

But John was struck dumb. He couldn't think of anything to say, and his mouth had locked shut anyway.

"Sit down," Tony said, pointing to all of them in turn.

They did as they were told, and as they got settled—if you could call it settled in their petrified state—something caught the cop's eye. John saw it happen. He was looking at something behind the couch Jimmy had been lying on.

John's guts sank deeper.

"What do we have here?" Tony asked as he pulled a bag out from behind the couch and began to unzip it, the menacing smile never leaving his face. "Got some drugs or—"

He stopped short as he gazed into the bag. His eyes seemed to light up.

"This just keeps getting better and better," Tony said as he pulled out a wad of bills.

It was John's share from the last job. He knew he was a fool for sticking it behind the couch, and he cursed himself for doing it. He'd been meaning to get a safe, but had always found something else to spend the money on.

*You fucking fool.*

"I don't fucking believe it," Tony said and looked up at them. "Bentley's Insurance out of Quitman. Last week. That was you?"

They all sat rock-like, their spines rigid, eyes distant. The look of those who were properly fucked.

But then, a strange thing had happened. Instead of putting them in cuffs or calling on his shoulder radio, Officer Tribianni stuffed the wad of bills into his pocket. The four of them stared stupidly and wide-eyed as he did this, their mouths in varying states of agape.

Tony grabbed a chair from the kitchen and brought it over to the center of the room, clunked it down, and faced them all. His menacing smile was still there and a gleam of something John couldn't quite place glinted in the man's eyes.

"I'm in," he had said, quite matter-of-factly.

John and Larry had stared at each other a moment, then looked back to the cop before them.

They didn't say anything.

"We clear on that, boys?" Tony asked. "I'm in. Next thing you pull, you call me. I'm a part of this now, and if you don't like that, or you try to fuck me on anything, you're all gone."

He looked over their faces for a few moments, finding no opposition at all. John and the others simply stared at him, awed.

"Whose car is it out there, anyway?" Tony asked after a full minute.

Larry, looking absurdly like a school boy, raised his hand.

"It's m-mine."

Tony nodded. "I'd get it out of town and sell that bitch for whatever you can get tomorrow. Buy something else. That shit is gonna be hot."

Then he stood, walked back to the bag of John's money, and pocketed another wad. No one moved to stop him.

"I'll be expecting a call," he said as he pulled a card from his breast pocket and jotted a number on the back. "This is my cell. If I don't hear from you in the next couple weeks, why, I imagine we're gonna have a breakthrough on our little homicide case tonight."

He moved to the door, stopping to lay a hand on John's shoulder and leaning close to his ear.

"See you soon, killer."

And that was how Tony joined their crew. John was, quite simply, fucked.

They all were.

# Chapter 8

Jimmy Hanson scratched at the crook of his elbow as he pulled into Larry's driveway. His headlights spilled onto the long drive, causing the grass to glow emerald in the shine of his high-beams, and his tires crunched over gravel and rock with a soft hiss.

Larry's car was out front, but the house was dark. It wasn't late yet, and Larry was something of a night owl. If he wasn't home, Jimmy would have expected him to be awake, either reading a book or poring over papers from work while CNN buzzed in the background, informing the world of what a horrible place it was and telling it what to be offended about this week.

But there was nothing. Not even a light on in the front hall. Even the porch light was off.

Jimmy pulled up to the front steps and killed his engine. His window was down, and he lit a cigarette before stepping out. After a long drag, he looked around, noticing for the first time that Brenda's car wasn't here.

*Probably out together,* he thought. *No big deal.*

But he knew better. His gut knew better. Larry wasn't answering calls and had dropped off their radar in the past couple days and a night out with his wife and kid was no kind of explanation. Not with the shit they were involved in. No way, no how.

He scratched at the crook of his arm again, feeling his nerves rattle inside his skin. He'd taken the pop about twenty minutes before in the parking lot of a gas station off I-30, and he was still flying high. It was good shit too. Top shelf ice. In fact, he was glad Larry appeared to not be home. He didn't want Larry to see him this way, his nerves jittery, his pupils pinpoints. That smacking thing his lips would do sometimes as if they had a mind of their own.

Still, it was possible Larry was in there, maybe sleeping, perhaps under the weather. Yeah, maybe that was it. If he was sick and Brenda was out, maybe he'd been too out of it to call them back. Especially if it was a fever.

But fever or not, Jimmy was cursing himself for taking the pop on the way to see Larry. Not that he felt he had much choice in the matter. The little demon-monkey had climbed up on his shoulder and smiled its crooked, fanged grin at him, and it just wouldn't fucking stop! The thing would stare at him with the devil's eyes and those horrible teeth. Oh, *God*, the teeth!

The pop was the only thing that would make it go away.

Jimmy dragged again on the cigarette and dug in his pocket. He pulled out a small, white pill. It was the last of a bar of Xanax, but he had another in the console of his car. He popped it into his mouth and began to chew. Maybe it would counter the ice just enough to make him cool. Cool enough to fool Larry anyway.

*Fat chance, fuck-stick.*

His teeth ground the Xanax in his mouth as he made his way towards the door, and he took a few more drags on his smoke. At the top of the stairs he flicked the butt into the yard, blew out the smoke through his nostrils, and reached for the doorknob.

The door was hanging open.

It was only an inch or so, which was why he hadn't noticed it sooner, but it was open. His hand hung there in space, like a paused movie, his fingers tingling with the ice and a species of excited dread.

Larry lived in the country, but he wasn't the type to leave his door hanging open. For as long as Jimmy had known him, every time he entered or exited a door—especially his own—he would jerk the door into the frame securely, then rattle it to make sure it had latched. It was a habit, and one Jimmy hadn't seen him fail to execute a single time, even when he'd been drinking.

This was wrong.

This was *all* wrong.

The dread in his fingers now spread to his chest and sat on him like a living creature. His breathing became shallow and forced. His heart began to pound in his chest and ears and he could feel the artery in his throat bulge with the excitement.

*Get out of here,* a voice in his head told him through the fog of drugs and panic. *Get the fuck out of here, now!*

But Jimmy ignored the voice. His hand, still hanging two inches from the door handle, floated up and his fingers pushed the door inward. It swung silently on its well-oiled hinges, revealing the dark mouth of the front hallway. Three feet beyond the door, there was nothing but pitch. Jimmy thought he could feel things in there, hiding in the dark, watching him. At one point he thought he saw the shadows move, as if they were a living thing, and the rational part of his brain, the one mostly deactivated from the ice and Xanax, was screaming at him from somewhere deep in the recesses of his consciousness that it was the drugs—*the drugs, god-dammit!*—that were creating those images. Nothing more.

But the rest of his mind, bathed in amphetamines and downers, said otherwise.

*Fuck me, it's the monkey! The god-damned demon-monkey! He's in there!*

Paralyzing fear kept him rooted in place as he stared into the abyss, feeling it stare back into him. Into his *soul*.

Then a voice, right in his ear, spoke up.

*"Go in, Jimmy-boy."*

It was the voice of the thing he thought was moving in the shadows. The awful demon-monkey with its fangs and apocalyptic eyes that spelled doom and destruction. Only it was on his back again, urging him forward, telling him to move. He thought he'd banished it for a short while with the pop, but here it was, and it wasn't going away.

*"Move."*

Jimmy gulped with a mouth that felt like sand, his body trembling, and stepped through the door. The house was very dark, and what little light there was coming through the windows from outside cast nightmare shapes about the room, ones that crawled and slinked, seeming to come towards Jimmy with their abominable, black fingers. But then they would recede and go back into the dark of the room.

His hand shot out, flipped the light switch next to the door.

The hallway flooded with light, casting the shadows out at once to the far corners of the house. He thought his heart slowed just a bit, enough so he could listen to the quiet of the house.

"L-Larry?" he stammered. "Larry, you home?"

The silence which answered him was absolute.

Jimmy took a few more steps into the house, his heartrate kicking up a tick, and his head was strained forward on his neck, cocked slightly askew so as to listen. Each step he took was a thunderous roar which seemed to be swallowed up by the quiet almost instantly.

"Larry?" he called again, quieter this time. The silence in the house seemed oppressive. "Larry, we've been trying to reach you. T-there's a problem and Johnny's wor—"

He stopped. He thought he had heard something, but he couldn't be sure. He froze, utterly still in the hallway, about halfway down, and realized he wasn't breathing. He was listening with all his might.

*Tick-tick-tick-tick.*

A mechanical sound, something further down, towards Larry's office. And there was something else too, something he couldn't identify at all. It was almost like...like...

*Smacking?*

He shook his head and remembered to breathe. The ticking sound came to him again, and his drug-addled brain identified it as the sound of Larry's grandfather clock, standing in the corner of his office. Then the smacking sound came again. Jimmy's eyes narrowed in confused wonderment at what he could possibly be hearing.

His heart thundered in his chest, threatening to one-up the

famous scene in 'Alien'. He gritted his teeth and forced his feet to move forward again, clomping down the hallway with soul-shredding loudness.

He neared the door to Larry's office, and a stench met his nostrils which nearly made him vomit up his Xanax. It was ripe and sweet, like turned lunchmeat. He gagged and clasped his hand over his mouth. His eyes pinched shut as he struggled to hold it together. After a moment, he began taking deep breaths through his mouth, trying to avert the smell, but it lingered in his mind and he began to think he could taste the odor in the air.

With an effort, he reached down to the handle of the door and twisted it open. Even though he was breathing from his mouth, the smell intensified at once, a monstrous and invisible cloud engulfing him from all sides, offending all five of his senses. His eyes stung and his skin mounded in gooseflesh.

But he couldn't see anything.

Like the rest of the house, this room was dark too. Only a little light spilled in from the hallway, revealing nothing but a couple feet of Larry's gray and red carpet. As Jimmy reached into the room, feeling for the light, a thought hit him, one from that deep recess in his mind where rational thought still lurked like a banished outcast.

*Larry's carpet is just...gray.*

A moment later, without thought, Jimmy flipped on the light.

The first scream came out as more of a hoarse grunt, his eyes bulging to their popping point. He began to double over, but his head stayed straight, looking at the horror before him. He heard an insane, cackling laughter from the demon-monkey, could hear its fangs gnashing next to his ear, could feel its hot, stinking breath on his skin.

Larry was in his chair, duct tape holding him to it by the arms and legs. There was a hole just above one eye, and a smattering of gore behind him. There seemed to be something protruding from his foot, and there was an awesome pool of blood encircling it there like a poorly painted pond. The blood was brown and crusty looking now, and Jimmy began to feel his stomach begin to recoil. This was all bad enough, but it was far from the worst part.

A woman sat to one side of Larry on the floor. She was upright and leaned against him, and Jimmy saw several fingers missing. But what really drew his attention was the flayed mouth of the woman, a sickening clown's grin stretching all the way back to the rear of her jaws.

*Tick-tick-tick-tick.*

The second scream came, and this time his voice found a little more traction. The woman was Brenda, and along with her missing fingers and the expansion of her mouth, he could see her throat was slashed.

Jimmy screamed long and hard as his eyes fell on the final and most fearsome horror this chamber held. It was Dylan, behind his parents and against his father's desk, his throat slashed as well. But it was the twin streams of dried blood which drooped from his empty eye-sockets which nearly sent Jimmy off the rails into complete madness.

*"Oh, God!"* he sobbed and hitched in breath for another scream.

In the split-second before he could let it out, he heard that other sound again, the unidentifiable smacking sound he'd heard before he'd stepped into hell itself, and his breath caught in his throat. He turned his head toward it, the ticking of the grandfather clock a maddening metronome of terror under the sound.

It was the cat. The god-damn, fucking cat. Jimmy's mind was too high and too reeling to place the little shit's name, but there it was, curled up on the floor away from his slaughtered owners, gnawing on something. Jimmy heard the thing purring loudly as it smacked away on its prize.

*Tick-smack-purr-tick-smack-purr-tick.*

Jimmy stumbled forward and fell to his knees a few feet from the cat. Its green eyes greeted him with all the warmth of Antarctica, and the thing hissed at him. He could hear the demon-monkey hissing and barking laughter in his ear, his mind swirling in and out of focus.

The cat was chewing on a finger. *Brenda's* finger, he concluded when he saw the giant diamond ring on it.

The furry bastard—*Snuggles, that was its name!*—went back to work on its snack as Jimmy got his feet under him and stumbled backwards into the ticking grandfather clock. The glass door which showed the pendulum swinging shattered and cut his arm, though he didn't feel it. He was still screaming, but he was unaware of anything now as he turned and ran down the hallway, spilled down the front steps onto his face, and scrambled into his car. He was still screaming when he managed to get the engine started and sped down the driveway. And then he screamed all the more when he looked into the rearview mirror. The monkey was in the backseat. And it was still laughing.

# Chapter 9

The phone's shrill ring woke John from his shallow, stress-induced nap with a gasp. He rubbed sleep from his eyes, inhaling deeply in an attempt to wake himself up, and reached for his chattering cell phone. He blinked blearily at the screen, trying to read the caller ID.

It was Jimmy.

He swiped his thumb and answered the call.

"Hello?" he croaked groggily.

"J-Johnny?" an apparently terrified Jimmy nearly screamed.

John flinched at the urgent bark of fear as though an icepick had come through the speaker and embedded itself in his ear. His heart quickened, and a sick feeling dropped in the bottom of his gut. Jimmy was a fuck-up, but Jimmy wasn't one to give into fear, not in all the years John had known him. Whatever was coiling itself around Jimmy's spine now had to be bad.

"Jimmy, what's—" John started, but Jimmy cut him off.

"Something bad happened, man!" Jimmy continued. "Oh, fuck, man! Oh, Jesus Ch—"

John was fully sitting up in his chair now, all traces of grogginess gone and his knuckles turning white as he grasped the phone. He stood, his eyes confused and squinted. He struggled to control his breath and speak calmly.

"What's going on, Jimmy?"

John heard what he thought were tires squealing and a pair of muffled curses. The sound of road noise droned from the phone.

"Jimmy, talk to me, god-dammit!" John shouted into the phone, trying to jar Jimmy out of his panic.

John heard heaving breaths on the line for a few moments and then Jimmy came back on, calmer now, starting to get hold of himself.

"It's Larry," he said, his voice calmer but wavering as though he might be crying. "He's dead, Johnny! I came out here–"

"He's *what?*" John hissed, his eyes saucers now. "*Dead?*"

A numbing terror coiled itself over him and he collapsed back into his chair. His mouth hung open, unbelieving.

*Dead? How could Larry be dead? What could have happened to him? He wasn't that old, he wasn't in perfect health but—*

Then darker thoughts encroached on his mind.

*No, it wasn't his health, you idiot. It wasn't his heart and he didn't have a stroke. You know what kind of life you guys are in. Sooner or later, things go bad. Sometimes you rip off the wrong people and you get the hard goodbye.*

"Yeah, oh God, man!" Jimmy was saying in his ear, audibly crying now. "I don't know what the hell to do! His face...ah, Jesus man, his fucking face was all smashed up and, and his b-b-brains are...fuck! Somebody worked him over, man. Worked him over hard. Blood everywhere. And Brenda and his kid, oh fu—"

"Brenda and Dylan are dead too?" John cut in with a strange species of shocked wonder in his voice.

"Jesus, man, are you hearing me?" Jimmy was screaming again. "They're dead! They're all dead! And Brenda's face, I...I can't even...and that poor kid, oh, god-dammit, Johnny! What do we do? What the fuck do we do, Johnny?"

John sat in stunned silence, pondering the rush of information he neither understood nor wanted to possess flooding his mind. Their situation had turned from one of confused frustration to nightmare bewilderment in the space of a moment. Larry—hell, his whole family—dead. Murdered. Tortured first, by the sound of it. Tony gone with the mon—

*Tony.*

Every job they'd ever done went off like greased lightning. No issues. Total proficiency. And the one thing all those jobs had in common was their mastermind. Larry. Now, one job in with slick-shit Tony calling the shots and the Horowitz family was dead and...

*...and Tony had walked out with everybody's money.*

Fucked didn't begin to approach the reality of what they were. Wasn't even in the same ballpark. Wasn't even the same fucking sport.Tony had bulldozed his arrogant-ass into their crew, and now had dragged them into something they didn't understand and weren't prepared for. There was no other explanation. The timing was too convenient for it to be a mere home invasion. No, this was payback. Recompense. A reckoning.

Somebody wanted their fucking money back.

"Shut the fuck up!" Jimmy screamed into the phone, but not at John. John hadn't said anything. Who the hell was with Jimmy?

"Who are you talking to?" John asked, his voice rising with his heart.

There was a beat of silence, then, "N-nobody, Johnny. Just the goddamn monkey...ah, fuck, it's nobody."

"If you've got someone with you I need to—"

"I just told you I don't! Now what the hell do we do?"

John blinked a few times, digesting everything and trying to keep it down. He decided to dismiss Jimmy's outburst and moved on.

"Jimmy, get over here. Right now, do you hear me? We have to talk. Put our heads together."

"You tell Tony, man, okay? I-I can't—"

"No, fuck that. And don't you call him either. You just come straight over here. Hold it together, drive like a blue-haired old lady, but get here. I think we've got other problems."

"What's happening, Johnny?" Jimmy asked, the tone of his voice that of a child's.

"I think we finally stirred the wrong pot. And we let ourselves get pulled right into it."

He hung up the phone, dropped it to the couch, then ran his fingers through his hair. He began to pace the room. After a few trips back and forth, he turned and started up the stairs. Halfway up, he realized Jenny was standing at the top of staircase, a concerned, solemn look on her face. She clutched the blanket from their bed tightly around her naked body.

"Did I hear 'dead', Johnny?" she asked, a small quiver in her bottom lip, her voice trembling. "Who's dead?"

John stared at her, his eyes beginning to sting. He didn't want to answer her. Perhaps, somehow, if he just didn't answer her question it would all go away. It wouldn't be true. As if the mere act of stating a fact out loud changed it from fiction to reality. But these were childish thoughts. Thoughts brought on by his old nemesis—fear—now taunting him as it clawed at his thrumming heart.

"Larry," he said, barely above a whisper.

A brief cry escaped her lips as she clasped a hand over her mouth.

"And," he went on in a choked voice, "Brenda and Dylan, too."

Tears welled in the corners of her eyes, her breath coming in hitches. The tears spilled from her widening eyes and she began to swoon. John thought she might collapse.

He climbed the remaining stairs to her two at a time and wrapped her in his arms. Her weight sagged against him and he pulled her in tight to his chest. As a terrible wail began to come from her, John's mind went to Tony, the bags in his hands as he flippantly walked away with all their money.

*You're a cunt, Savage,* he had said. *You ain't doing nothing about it.*

But Tony was wrong about John.

*Oh, you motherfucker,* John thought. *We're doing something about it, you can put that shit in the bank.*

Jenny wept on John's shoulder as a single tear spilled over his cheek. Even still, the budding of a dark smile touched his lips.

# Chapter 10

Mr. Spears sat in the passenger seat of the black Mercedes. His boys were inside the house of a man named Jimmy Hanson. A cursory sweep of the place had revealed he wasn't home, but that was of little consequence. Of course, he had every intention of catching up with Hanson, the dirty cop Tribbiani, and the Savage character. There was recompense due, and there was a bag in the trunk with a two pound hammer and a handful of railroad spikes which would reap the rewards for him nicely.

For starters, anyway.

But for now, they were looking for the cash. The cash which had disappeared from his own home not five days prior. And he meant to find it.

*There's fucking up, and then there's fucking up. And you boys fucked up.*

Indeed they had.

Spears was a skilled tradesman. His trade typically consisted of solving problems for others, and he was rewarded handsomely for his services. If you had a rat you couldn't seem to shoo, Alexander Spears was the man you called. If you had a threat against you, Alexander Spears was the man you called. If you needed information extracted, he had the tools to pull it out. If your wife was guzzling cum from your asshole of a business partner, well...

Spears was the guy.

He was the problem solver. He was the dog you sent after the scent. He had contacts all over the place. He had three others he worked with on a regular basis, though his most apt pupil, Doug, was attending to other business just then. Their clientele consisted of small-time hoods, powerful gangsters, politicians, and absurdly—yet nevertheless true—the elder board of a large church. He had spent some years building his little empire, socking away cash where he could, and maintaining absolute discretion.

But these small-time assholes had stolen it. They took his cash right out of his goddamned home while he'd been away on business. The money was bad enough, but the blatant disrespect of the thing is what bothered him the most. In all his years, the thing which had set him apart from others in his line of work—and the thing which he believed had kept him alive and in one piece—was his determination to treat his clients *and* his prey with respect. It was essential. Respect kept you cool. When people were cool, things didn't get out of hand. When things didn't get out of hand, you didn't get caught.

This was the first time he had ever been ripped off.

The very thought of it caused molten lava to course through his system. He looked down and noticed for the first time his hands were clenched into fists, the skin on his knuckles stretched tight and drained of color. He forced his hands to open, the fingers aching from the strain. He also noticed his teeth were grinding against one another, threatening to turn themselves to powder. He unclenched his jaw, took a deep breath, then sighed as he let it out, pinching his eyes shut in frustration.

He would kill the insolent fools who'd taken his money. He would kill them good, too. Make an example out of them. Put the word out about what happened when people treated Alexander Spears with disrespect.

His thoughts turned to the cop who had been snooping around his business a few weeks back. The cop—a detective with the Dallas PD called Jantz—had come around to his house. Started asking questions Spears hadn't liked. Hadn't liked one bit. They were questions related to some work he'd recently done for one of his clients, and by some miraculous misfortune, this cop had zeroed in on Spears as a 'person of interest'.

"I know your business, Spears," Jantz had said when Spears had stopped answering his questions. "There's a whole slew of these murders around. You're good, I'll give you that. I don't have anything I can charge you with, but I will. And when I do, you're going to want me to be your friend. See, I'm good at that. Being a friend, I mean. But there's something else I'm just as good at. You know what that is?"

Spears had merely stared at the man, a cold, icy glare which he'd mastered through his years of work.

"That's okay, I'm putting you on the spot," Jantz went on with an arrogant wave of the hand. "I'll just tell you. I'm also good at being your worst fucking nightmare."

Spears had swallowed, working hard to make it invisible, and softened his gaze. Just a bit.

"What do you want?" Spears had asked.

Jantz smiled at this and chuckled quietly.

"Well," he started, dragging the word out. "I know with the kind of work you do, you're well paid. But I've checked your accounts. Got a buddy who's not too particular about warrants and all. But your accounts don't show all that much. Someone with your, uh, *skills* I would think you'd have a lot more stashed away. But it ain't in your bank, that's for sure."

Jantz was silent for a few moments, his hands working neatly into his trousers. There was the faintest cocking of the man's eyebrow, just slightly upturned, and the hint of a smile at the corner of his mouth which Spears had found unforgiveable. But he maintained his cool, because that's what professionals did.

"How much?" he asked the cop.

Jantz had shrugged, pursing his lips in an animated gesture, and said, "Oh, I guess we could start with about ten."

*Start.*

The word—never mind its implications—hadn't been lost on Spears.

Spears had smiled and moved to the triptych of Bosch's *The*

*Garden of Earthly Delights* and removed the middle panel. Opened his safe. Fished out a wrapped stack, the printing on the band stating: Ten-Thousand Dollars. He closed the safe and spun the combination, then turned back to the man. Jantz had been leaning forward, as though he'd been looking into the safe over Spears's shoulder, but was quickly recovering and rocking on his heels.

Spears held up the money.

"Here," he said and dropped it on his desk before the man. "Are we done now?"

Jantz snatched up the stack, fanned the bills, and sniffed them. Then he'd laughed as he dropped the money into the pocket of his blazer.

"For now," he said, then winked at Spears.

Then he left.

There were no more questions, and Spears had gone on about his work like normal. A month later, a similar meeting had occurred with Jantz once more, and once more, Spears had paid the man. Normally he'd have just killed him and melted his body in acid and been done with it, but he thought perhaps he could use the cop for protection. From time to time, protection was a handy thing to have.

This had proved to be Spears's greatest miscalculation.

The day he'd come in and found the safe raided, he had gotten Vic and Paul and went straight to the detective's residence. He had found where the man lived immediately after their first meeting, and found the man had a wife and two daughters. He had filed all of this away for later use, should the occasion arise.

And now it had.

When Jantz had come in after ten that night, smelling of booze and swaying slightly on his feet, Spears had been waiting for him. Jantz's wife and two daughters were tied to chairs with duct tape, their faces streaked with tears and snot. Their mouths were all stuffed with cloth and taped over, and their moans drifted through the house like the voices of ghosts.

"Have a seat, detective," Spears had said.

The man's eyes were wide and his breathing shallow, but he'd done as Spears had commanded. He sat on the couch opposite his three girls, hands shaking.

"L-look, you don't have to—"

Jantz stopped as Spears produced a silenced pistol from his coat and blew the brains out of Mrs. Jantz. Gore had blasted from her head as she toppled over, still taped to the chair, and Jantz hissed a wheezing scream. The two children in their own chairs were moaning now, their eyes bulging and terrified, and Spears had stepped between them. He laid a hand on one girl's shoulder and the pistol on the other girl's. Jantz seemed to tighten up, freezing on the couch, and locked eyes with Spears.

"Now that I have your attention," Spears said in a calm, icy voice, "let's get down to business. I was robbed. We both know it was you, or someone you're associated with, so let's dispense with the bullshit. Where is it, or where can I find it? I need a name."

He made a come on gesture with his free hand and cocked an ear towards the detective.

There was stammering and weeping, and Vic and Paul had busted the man's nose and those of his two daughters, and still the man continued to beg. For such a tough guy, he hadn't been very smart.

Spears emptied the head of the man's youngest daughter, her gray matter speckling Jantz's face, and that had gotten through. Though only barely. The man still only gave up a single name, and when it became clear he wasn't going to give up more, even after his last remaining daughter was on the floor with a gaping head wound, Spears had decided one name would have to do.

Then he'd crucified the man to the wall with spikes.

*Horowitz.* That was the only name he'd gotten, and, as it turned out, the only one he'd needed. Horowitz had been plenty willing to sing once Spears showed him the tune, and he'd sung perfectly on key.

There was another cop in the mix, though. That was the real connection. But from Spears's research, it seemed Horowitz was the big cheese of this little group, and if there was a weak link in their pathetic chain it was this character Hanson. He was a junkie.

And junkie's caved.

They talked. They rolled over when you pushed. So it was here Spears had decided to start.

He wasn't happy about the late start, but he also didn't want to start making splashes in such a small town when all the lights were on in the homes on every street. They'd gone by the other cop's place first. There were lights on inside, and the flicker in the windows from a TV told Spears the man was up. He wasn't worried about dealing with the cop, but if he could get the Hanson junkie to spill some more information, he'd go in better armed than he was now.

He had seen shadows moving as the cop moved between rooms, fetching beers *(probably bought with my fucking money!)* and a bag of Doritos, or whatever the fuck cops snacked on at night.

They'd sat on the house for some time, then moved on to the place Savage lived. Lights were on here as well, but he could see people milling about inside, both upstairs and down, through the windows donning the front of the apartment. And a condo apartment was no good to rush into. It wasn't the place to do it.

The junkie's house was dark and quiet. There was a large yard with a gentle incline coming up from the street level to a small peer and beam house with vinyl siding. By the time they'd arrived, it had reached the later hours and most of the houses on the street were dark and quiet. Winnsboro had roughly thirty-five-hundred residents, but you wouldn't have known a single other person was in town by looking at the street that night.

He stepped out of the car which he had parked down the street from the house and strolled casually to the abode of Jimmy Hanson, glancing over his shoulders twice, confirming all was still quiet.

It was.

"Anything?" he asked in a gravelly voice after he'd shut the door.

"Not a damn thing, boss," said Vic, the bigger of his two guys. "If he's got it, it ain't here."

Spears twisted his neck in frustration, tendons creaking and bones popping back into alignment.

"Alright," Spears said, his eyes pinched shut in thought. "We'll wait for him. He's got to come home eventually. We'll have him show us. Maybe persuade him a little."

Spears produced what might have been some sort of unholy abomination of a smile, his lips peeling back over his yellowing teeth. Vic and Spears's smaller guy, Paul, nodded, glancing at each other momentarily.

Spears dropped the bag from the car with the hammer and spikes on the table. There was a loud *thunk* as it settled. Then he pulled his .45 from his waist, checking the magazine and slamming it back into place. He racked the slide, chambering a round, and flipped the safety on. Then he reached into the pocket of his jacket and produced a sound suppressor, which he promptly began screwing onto the end of the barrel.

Vic and Paul did the same.

# Chapter 11

The god-damn, fucking *monkey*!

It was back there, cackling away with its sinister, idiot bark, the fangs bared in a horrifying, clownish grin, the black eyes glistening wet.

*"Ee-ahh! Ha ha ee! Ahh-ee HA!"* the terrible thing cackled.

"Shut the fuck up!" Jimmy roared as his car rolled into the city limits of Winnsboro.

His flesh felt clammy, and his vision kept blurring. He wiped at his eyes and tried to dry his sweating hands on his jeans. It was no good.

*Too much Xanax,* he thought.

But he could fix that. And fuck Johnny if he asked anything about it. He could take his sanctimonious attitude and shove it straight up his snotty ass. And then some.

*"Ahh-ee he ha!"* the thing continued tormenting him.

The monkey had first started coming around back when he'd been on heroin. After his third or fourth pop, the thing had arrived. It was smaller then, not much like it was now. There were no fangs, the eyes had some color to them, the fur wasn't a matted nightmare. It was kinder too. It would talk to him, a thing which had both horrified and mesmerized Jimmy at the same time the first time it happened. It gave him advice. Told him what to try.

This advice proved to be ill-advised all around more times than not, but that was no matter. Jimmy Hanson had never made many wise choices in his relatively short life. What were a few more?

But then the thing got bigger. It got uglier. It got meaner. Instead of the cute, innocent looking animal it had been at first, it turned into a malicious demon of a chimpanzee. Fangs had begun sprouting in place of its teeth. The pupils of its eyes had begun to widen ever more, eventually obliterating all else and leaving it with the twin coals it now sported. The hair got dirtier and the thing stunk. No more did it show up when he was high—though this may have been because of the difference between heroin and speed—but when he wasn't. When he was jonesing for a hit, suddenly it was there, on his god-damn back, its rancid breath in his ear telling him things, awful things, *evil* things.

Then Jimmy would take a pop and the thing would go away for a while. But he came back.

He *always* came back.

Now things were changing, though. Now the thing seemed to be here all the time. Wasted or stone sober, it didn't matter. It was *there*.

"Would you just go away!" Jimmy screamed, looking into his rearview at the awful thing.

Its laughing stopped then. The black eyes moved wetly in its sockets, the remnants of its smile fading around its fangs. Yellowed, filthy fangs.

Something about this transformation chilled Jimmy. His spine tingled. Goose-flesh rippled his arms and sweat broke from his brow. It was just staring at him now, a look of indifference or malevolent loathing on its face, he couldn't tell which. All he knew was the thing was scaring him now.

*"Watch out,"* the thing said.

Jimmy squinted his eyes in wonderment at this before hearing a car horn blaring at him. He realized he'd drifted into the other lane while staring at the demon monkey in the back seat. Headlights filled the windshield and Jimmy swerved hard back onto his side, narrowly missing the other car. It kept its horn blaring a moment longer, fading behind him now, and Jimmy pulled his car to the shoulder and threw it in park. He was shaking. He was sweating. He was cold.

He needed a fix.

The thing in the back continued to stare. Jimmy forced himself to look away from it and went for the glove box. He found his stuff, got it ready. He wrapped a belt around his arm, found the vein, and began to soar.

He exhaled with ecstasy as he released the belt and threw all his shit in the passenger seat. He took several deep breaths, feeling the surge in his body, feeling his heart begin to race, feeling motherfucking *alive*!

*Oh, yeah, bitch.*

Suddenly there was a whisper in his ear. The thing from the back seat, rancid decay on its breath, but Jimmy didn't care now. He could deal with anything when he was flying, and friends and neighbors, he was flying now.

He listened to the thing. It told him horrible things. Depraved things. Things he didn't believe, at least not at first. But the thing was compelling. It was reasoning. Why shouldn't he believe Johnny and the others were planning to cut him out? Why else would Johnny be so far up his ass about being on the shit? He'd been on him about that for years now, even for that short while he'd been clean. Constantly bugging him and watching him and god-damn judging him! Was there ever an end to it? Ever?

No. There wouldn't be. Not until Johnny cut Jimmy out. And Jenny, that teasing slut. Jimmy knew her type. She wanted to get your cock hard but never wanted you to put it in her. She was just like Johnny. The questions, the fucking judgmental stares if he seemed a little off. It was in her voice too when she was on the phone. That *oh, you pitiful little thing, you* tone that he hated, hated, *HATED!* And don't even let him get started about Tony...

The thing had some good points, Jimmy had to admit that. But then, he always had thought the thing made good points. He'd always listened to it once he got flying. If things turned out badly, that was Jimmy's fault for fucking it up, not the chimp's. A good plan could still be executed poorly.

He took another deep breath, relishing the rotten smell of the thing's breath as it continued to tell him what he ought to do. What he *should* do. He could get the drop Johnny, even Tony too if the timing was right. Maybe even give Jenny a nice dip from Jimmy's big cock. Cut her tits off after. Stupid bitch.

He popped a half a tab of Xanax and chewed it like bitter candy. He needed to bring himself down just a little bit. The thoughts he was having, the thoughts the thing was putting into his mind, they weren't him. They weren't him at all. But even as he tried to reason this, he thought again of taking them out. Of murder and rape and mutilation. And his dick got hard.

He put the car in drive and pulled back on the road. All the while the monkey was still whispering in his ear.

# Chapter 12

Jimmy came into John and Jenny's apartment with a sheen of sweat on his face. John took one look at him and narrowed his eyes. He was high. John knew it. And on closer inspection, his assumption was confirmed. Jimmy's pupils were tiny dots in the center of his eyes.

*Not heroin,* John thought, *but he's on some shit.*

Jimmy was also crying. He was twitching nervously, looking over his shoulder at the wall, a species of fear and angst on his face which put John ill at ease.

"God-damnit, Jimmy," John said with a sigh.

Jimmy glanced up at him, trying poorly to appear as though he was unaware of what John was referring to.

But he knew. John could see right through him.

"Wh-what are you—" Jimmy started, but John cut him off.

"The fuck is the matter with you?" John hissed, getting right in his face. "Everything's falling apart and you're soaring! I told you I needed you strai—"

Now it was Jimmy's turn to cut John off.

"Back the *fuck* off!" Jimmy yelled. "I Just saw one of my best friends fucking mutilated, do you get that?"

John's features softened ever so slightly. "I get it—"

"No you fucking don't! I'm not your god-damned kid, I'm not your ward, so shut your damn mouth!"

John had never seen Jimmy like this before, and his words had caused him to take a step back, the rage on his face replaced with unease. Jimmy seemed to soften a moment later, took a deep breath through his tears. Then he did a strange thing. He put his hands over his ears and began shaking his head, whispering the word *"no"* over and over again for several moments. Then his hands were at his side and he was looking, no, *glaring* over his shoulder at the wall.

"Shut up!" Jimmy hissed in a whisper.

John had no idea what was going on with him, but it wasn't the time to deal with Jimmy's mental breakdown. He turned from Jimmy without another word and pulled his phone from his pocket. They needed to move, to get out. He had been trying to get hold of Tony. Tony, who had the money. Tony, who had the badge. Tony, who had the attitude.

Tony, who had set the whole thing up.

John hadn't reached him. He wasn't exactly surprised by this, but it did nothing to calm his agitation. His nerves tingled in his extremities and his breathing was forced and labored. Pain stabbed in the center of his forehead as if an ice pick were wedged between his eyes and a phantom hand were twisting it.

*Pull it together. Calm down. We can deal with this, we just need to cool our heads and think.*

Tony was a motherfucker. That was the word commonly used to describe cops on the take. Motherfucker. And after the interaction with Tony earlier, Jimmy's phone call about Larry, and a little time to think and put things in perspective, John was getting the nagging feeling that their particular motherfucker was busy about the business of fucking them out of their money.

The call went to voicemail. Again.

"God-dammit!" John hissed as his thumb angrily tapped the touch screen on his phone.

Jimmy's face was pale, and his Adam's apple bobbed up and down as though a hungry fish were taking the bait below it.

"We have to get out of here," John snapped. "We need to load up, find Tony and the money, and get the fuck out of here for a while."

Jimmy was obviously frightened, but nodded his head. He was shaking, his skin pale and pasty, sheening with sweat. John thought he looked as though he'd aged ten years. Lines in Jimmy's face that John could not recall being there stood out starkly about his sunken, dark eyes.

As John beheld his withering old friend, his eyes drifted down and he noticed the blood on Jimmy's arm.

"Wha—"

Then he noticed the revolver stuffed into his waistband.

"Holy shit, Jimmy!" John exclaimed. "What the hell is going on?"

Jimmy looked about the room as though he wasn't sure where he was. Confusion and terror seemed to saturate his face, and his moist eyes seemed unable to focus.

"Jimmy?" John asked. "Jimmy, what the fuck happened to your arm?"

Several more seconds of the confused eye-darting continued, then Jimmy's eyes found John's. They focused and grew worried. His mouth moved a few times, but nothing came out. His throat clicked audibly.

John crossed the room to him and grabbed his shoulders. He locked eyes with Jimmy and took a few deep breaths, trying to get Jimmy to match his breathing.

It worked.

"Jimmy, I need you to talk to me," John said in a measured and soothing voice. "What happened?"

Another click from Jimmy's throat as his Adam's apple bobbed. He finally found his voice.

"I-I don't know, man," he said just above a whisper. "W-When I f-found Larry and..."

Fresh tears streamed his face, and once more he looked over his shoulder, his face scrunched as if he were listening to someone speaking. Then his eyes came back to John's.

"I-I backed into that clock," he went on. "You know the one, in Larry's office? Big fucking thing. I was freaking out, man. I gashed it and...and I..."

"And you got the hell out of there," John finished for him, dropping his hands from Jimmy's shoulders and nodding. "I don't blame you. I'm sorry you had to see that."

"So god-damn awful," Jimmy sobbed, looking at a point on the floor. "His wife, Johnny, she was...and the fucking kid. Who would do something like that?"

John turned from him and stared at the screen of his phone, which still showed Tony's number as the last dialed.

"Somebody bad," John said, locking the screen of his phone. It made a digital *click*. "Somebody real fucking bad. We never should have gone along with this. With Tony. We have a routine and we fucked with that and now it's biting us in the ass."

"God-damn you!" Jimmy suddenly hissed and John whirled around to face him. "Leave me alone!"

Jimmy was facing the wall now, fists clenched, staring at nothing. But the look on his face showed he *was* seeing someone. Or some*thing*.

John looked again to the gash on Jimmy's arm and he reached out and pulled up the sleeve. It was a relatively minor wound, nothing that would need stiches, but what John saw all around the gash caused his breath to catch in his throat.

Jimmy hadn't seemed to notice John pull his sleeve up. He was still whispering curses at the wall and mumbling things John couldn't make out. But he wasn't focused on that. He was focused on the pockmarks all around the crook of Jimmy's elbow. Needle tracks.

Jimmy was on some shit, but it wasn't the shit he'd kicked a couple years back. Heat seemed to come off Jimmy in waves, and as he held his friend's arm, John could feel the man's pulse. It was racing into the stratosphere.

Jimmy then brought his other hand to his mouth and popped something. Began chewing. Brittle, crunching sounds issued from his face, and he seemed to come out of the raging fugue he'd just been in. John let go of his arm. He wanted to punch him. Wanted to fucking kill him. But he also felt sorry for him. Jimmy's life had been hard, anyway.

And now, after finding Larry and his family as he had, he wondered if he might not do the same if he'd traveled Jimmy's road. There was such pain in Jimmy's eyes. There was fear, too, yes, but so much pain. Genuine agony.

Jimmy's eyes wandered away into that unfocused wasteland once again and John took a few steps away from him. Jimmy was dredging his hands over his scalp and his fingers ran through his hair, clutching great swaths of it in his fists.

Jimmy began to cry then. Hitching sobs escaped him, his hands stuck to his temples. John looked once more to the gun in Jimmy's waistband and considered trying to get it from him. The man was coming apart at the seams, cursing at walls, on some sort of shit. But going for it might backfire. He didn't want that.

John had to sit down. Had to *think*. Things were so far beyond fucked, he couldn't see straight. They'd tripped a wire somewhere and now landmines were going off all around them. Ripping through them. What in God's name had they done? Who had they ripped off? What had Tony gotten them into?

All these questions had to be answered. Had to be answered soon. But where to start?

*Tony.*

John's eyes snapped up. John leaned forward and put a hand on Jimmy's shoulder as Jimmy sat down across from him, eyes lost and swirling.

"Jimmy?" he asked.

"Yeah," Jimmy whimpered, his voice cracking as he said it. He sounded like a scared little boy.

"I need you to pull yourself together," John said in an even and soothing tone. "We have to find Tony."

"Where's the money?" Jimmy asked.

John looked up where he had set the money before Tony had come and taken it. Gone now, only God knew where.

*And Tony.*

"Tony took it," John replied.

Jimmy's glistening eyes met John's, confused wonder in them.

The pinpricks of his pupils caught the light and shone.

"We never should have gotten in bed with that motherfucker," Jimmy whispered, a tinge of horror in his voice.

Jimmy was right. Tony and his dirty cop pal in Dallas had stumbled into something very bad, and like fools led to the slaughter, all of them had followed along. It was so much money.

But now they were dealing with whoever was on the losing end of the heist, and whoever that was, they were pissed.

Pissed off and coming for them.

They had already gotten to Larry, and took out his whole family for good measure. He didn't know how, but that was irrelevant. The level of evil it took to do what they had done to the Horowitz family was staggering. What *was* relevant, however, was whether Larry had given the rest of them up before meeting his doom.

The thought terrified him to his core.

"We have to get out of here," John said, standing up. "Right now."

He left Jimmy weeping in the chair and went up to his and Jenny's room. He woke her, told her what was happening, and then went to his closet. He shifted things around on the top shelf and found the box he was looking for. He pulled it down, holding it in his hands as though it were some sacred relic. Or perhaps some fragile, glass bottle containing a toxic pathogen.

He lay it on the end of their bed, as gently as if handling old dynamite sweating nitroglycerin. He lifted the lid and exhaled a loud, exasperated breath.

Inside was the 9mm Beretta he'd shot the junkie with in the house where he'd found Jimmy all those years before. He'd put it away in this box after Tony had cornered them and barged his way into their operations, and he'd never touched it again. He'd not wanted anything to do with it, but he couldn't chance it going out on the street. Someone could have used it, and the ballistics might have drawn attention to the murder of the man in the crack house John had killed. Nothing Tony could do for him then, not that the motherfucker had any loyalty to them anyway.

John stared at the pistol for a long moment. It seemed to sneer at him, to mock him.

*Wanna play with me again, Johnny-boy? We had such a good time our last go around!*

John pinched his eyes shut, trying to force the thoughts away, instead focusing on the sounds of panties and shirt sliding over Jenny's flesh as she got dressed. He thought about the possibility of taking someone's life once more. He had never wanted to be faced with this again. He had no doubt he could do it, and that was perhaps the scariest part of the whole thing to him. His knowledge that he could do it. *Would* do it, if the situation forced him to. His old enemy was back.

Fear.

And it was winking at him.

He shuddered.

John opened his eyes and snatched up the Beretta. The grip fell into his hand like an old friend. Like it had never been absent.

*Getting the band back together, eh, Johnny-boy?*

He ignored the mocking voice and grabbed two fully loaded magazines from the box. He slammed one home in the gun and dropped the other in his jacket pocket. Then he chambered a round. The action worked flawlessly, sliding home like butter.

He gently put the hammer down, then shoved the gun into the back of his pants. As he did this, he looked up and saw Jenny staring at him. She was dressed now, her arms crossed beneath her bosom, her face drawn with worry and...

*And fear. Your old enemy has her now, too.*

"I'm sorry," he said, tears stinging his eyes.

She smiled at him and shook her head. She said nothing, only grabbed her coat and stepped towards him. She kissed him tenderly, cupping his face in her hand.

"I know, Johnny."

They went downstairs without another word. Jimmy was there, more composed than he'd been before. He told Jenny what he'd told John earlier, her face drawing more and more fearful with every word.

"Before we go," Jimmy said, turning to John as he finished his story, "I gotta swing by my place and get Roscoe."

Roscoe was Jimmy's dog. The *last* thing they needed to be sticking their necks out for was a fucking dog, in John's estimation. His face pinched together in frustration.

"Forget about the damn dog, Jimmy," John started with a dismissive wave of the hand. "We've got more important things to worry about than that mutt."

"I'm getting my goddamned dog, Johnny!" Jimmy said with finality. "I'll meet you guys at the motel as soon as I have him. I promise."

An argument could have ensued, but John wasn't up for it. Love of pets was a thing he didn't personally get, but he knew it was a reality, and not one he could bring down with reason. He relented, but stated they would go together and get the dog. He didn't feel it was safe to split up, even for just a few minutes.

"We'll get the mutt after we swing by Tony's," John said.

"Tony's?" Jimmy asked, his face contorting with concern. "Why the fuck we going to his place? He's the one who got us into all—"

"Because Tony has the fucking money, god-dammit!" John barked, more harshly than he'd intended. "There was no reason to clean the money, but he insisted, and with all that's going on, we need to get it and get out of here for a while. You already know all of this. Jesus, what the hell are you on?

Jimmy just glared at John, then twitched, as if someone had grabbed his ear. Then his head was half turned, and nodded as if in agreement. Jenny's eyes met John's with bewilderment. "What the hell is going on?" Jenny whispered to John as Jimmy continued to nod along to an invisible being.

"There's no time to talk about it. We need to move."

John snapped in front of Jimmy's face, jerking him out of his fugue.

"We're leaving."

Jimmy nodded and smiled at John in a way he'd never seen before. It was humorless and malevolent, something out of a horror movie, and it seemed to drain all the heat out of the room.

Then Jimmy nodded. "After you," he said.

John turned to the door, feeling the butt of his pistol brush against his back. Then he thought of the gun in Jimmy's waistband.

Gooseflesh erupted all over him as they stepped into the night.

# Chapter 13

Spears saw the dog a moment after it started barking. Barking at *him*. The sound startled him, and he drew in a quick, truncated breath as he turned.

He was in the dark living room, at the edge of a hallway. He jerked his head around and could see into the kitchen. There, directly across the kitchen from the hall was a door leading out the side of the house. Low and in its center, a swinging doggie door stood, its flap now sitting atop a brown mongrel baring its teeth. Slobber drooled from its fangs and a low growl purred between its barks.

*Fucking dogs.*

Spears hated dogs. He hated their smell, their noise, their proximity. They had no sense of personal space, no brain to think for themselves, and worst of all, male and female alike, they invariably tried to perform fellatio on him.

And they barked.

Sweet Christ on His throne, they *barked.*

It was the most horrid noise in the known universe. Why in hell anyone would want some smelly, noisy, blow-jobbing mutt in their home was something he would never understand.

He *loathed* them.

Even Anthony White's Dobermans—George and Mack they were called—were an utter nuisance. He avoided going to that client's place as often as possible. But at least in the case of George and Mack there was a purpose served. They had big, sharp teeth, and they knew how to guard and fight. But with this dog, and the vast majority of canines the world over, their existence and ownership was based on companionship.

*Companionship.*

*I'll never understand it,* he thought as pulled his silenced pistol from its holster under his coat.

The dog moved then, sliding into the house through its door, the flap swinging back and out like a pendulum. The animal never ceased its growls and barks and snarls. It didn't seem to be a very fierce beast, some sort of mutt from the look of it, but it was going the extra mile to put on a show now.

It came down the hall towards him, the barks increasing in frequency and volume. Louder. And louder.

And louder.

That was quite enough. Spears lifted his pistol with an exasperated sigh and drove a round into the thing's skull. The silencer cancelled most of the roar of the fired round, but there was still a sharp clap which popped in the narrow hallway. There was a brief, shrill yelp from the dog as it collapsed to the floor and then it was quiet again. The corner of Spears's lip curled up ever so slightly as he watched the thing's blood blossom around it.

*Ah, the beauty of silence. Is there anything better?*

Vic came into the room, his eyes wide and his gun out. He'd heard the shot. His eyes darted around a moment before he noticed the dog lying on the floor.

"The fuck happened?" Vic asked, his face contorted with confusion.

"I hate dogs, Victor," Spears started, re-holstering his gun. "They are a disease. They are filthy. They are annoying. They don't even cover their feces after a bowel movement."

Now he looked at Vic, as well as Paul, who'd just come up behind them. Disgust literally oozed from Spears's face like puss from a festering wound.

"They just leave it there to rot," he went on, his hand gesturing before him at an imagined scene. Then he lowered his hand and his eyes snapped back to theirs, locked. "And they bark. God-damn them, they bark. Cats, now," he waved a finger in the air, his eyebrows raising, "Cats are fine animals. They clean themselves, cover their fecal debris, and their mewing is at least tolerable."

Vic and Paul stared at him for a moment, blinking stupidly, mouths hanging open.

"I got a dog," Paul finally said.

Vic's eyes tightened in confused awe as his head turned to look at Paul. Spears might have smiled, but he wasn't about to soften his persona to his guys. He liked them scared. He liked them frightened. Frightened people didn't turn on you.

"What?" Vic half whispered, near horrified awe in his tone.

Paul looked dully at him a moment and shrugged. Vic shook his head and looked back to Spears.

"Find anything?" Spears asked, changing the subject.

Vic blinked a few times then shook his head.

"N-naw," he started with a stutter, then gulped. "Nothing."

Paul just shook his head, his shoulders rising in another idiot shrug.

"Keep looking," Spears said and turned to look back down at the dog, his smile returning. "Somebody has to come home eventually. Then we'll ask them where it is. Real nicely."

They pattered out of the hallway and resumed their search in the dark house. Spears continued staring at the dog, his grin ever widening. After a long moment, he whispered to himself.

"Oh, so nicely."

He kicked the dog.

# Chapter 14

*Are they out of their fucking minds?* Jimmy thought as he followed John and Jenny in their new WRX. *What do they think—*

The thing in the back seat was suddenly in his ear again, a cackling, maniac laugh erupting from its rancid mouth.

*"Ee-ah-he-he!"* it chortled.

It startled Jimmy and his hand jerked on the wheel, causing him to swerve. A fresh crop of sweat grew on his forehead, and he harvested it with his shirt sleeve as he got the car under control.

"What the fuck are you?" he screamed at the thing, looking at its horrible face in the rearview. "Why don't you leave?"

The thing's cackles stopped at once, its lips and cheeks drooping down not quite enough to conceal its razor fangs, the black eyes in its sockets dead, yet horrifyingly electric.

*"They're cutting you out, Jimmy,"* it said, the voice an aberration of sound. *"And you're going along with it."*

Jimmy's hands tightened on the wheel. He could feel the amphetamine in his veins, pumping at incredible velocity through his thrashing heart. His mouth twitched and his head jerked. At some point he became aware his breathing was fast and shallow, almost hyperventilating.

*Get a grip,* he thought to himself.

*"Yeah, get a grip,"* the thing said as if in response to his thought.

The breath caught in Jimmy's throat. The thing could hear his thoughts. That was obvious now. There was literally no escape from it, and it was alive with him and in him and always around. He couldn't shut it up! Shut it up! *SHUT! IT! UP!*

Jimmy began screaming then, a raging, horrible sound from deep in the gut. He felt his mind breaking apart and he wanted more ice. He wanted more pills. He wanted to fly. He wanted to be even. He wanted to feel good, feel sober, but he wanted the fucking venom inside him, too.

He was right on the tail of John and Jenny, mere inches behind them, dangerously close. He screamed again. His heart was thrumming in his ears, a near constant, booming hum.

The thing was there too, in his ear, whispering obscenities, verbal atrocities about what was happening to him. And he knew it was true. It was all god-damn true. They *were* cutting him out! The bitch and the asshole, right along with the motherfucker. All of them. In it together. They had worked this whole thing out together, probably killed Larry themselves. And the sick fucks sent *him* out there to find the bodies!

*"Mother-FUCKER!"* Jimmy roared at the windshield.

Then his phone was ringing. The digital chimes tingling through the tinny speaker and he glanced down at the screen as he snatched it up.

It was John.

*"They can't know you know,"* the monster he couldn't get off his back said into his ear. *"They'll ambush you."*

Jimmy was nodding, sweat exploding out of him now. He flipped the air conditioning on full blast before answering the call.

"Yeah?" he said in a voice much calmer than he'd thought manageable in his current state.

"Back the fuck off," John's voice barked from the tiny speaker. "We've got enough trouble without you drawing attention to us."

It was the first time it really registered how close he'd been tailgating the Subaru and he eased off his own accelerator.

"I'm getting my dog," Jimmy said after he'd settled back a comfortable distance. "I'm not interested in—"

"I told you we'll go together, god-dammit!" John roared at him. "But we have to get to Tony right now, I just need you to calm the fuck down."

"I bet you do," Jimmy whispered, his knuckles white on the phone's chassis.

"What was that?" John asked, a tone indignation rising in his voice. "The fuck did-"

"Nothing," Jimmy said, keeping the cool, even tone. "We'll get Roscoe after Tony."

The thing was whispering in one ear as John spoke into the other through the phone. It was telling Jimmy to keep it cool, don't give too much away. A good story could get spoiled if you gave too much away too soon. Gotta keep some mystery. Build the suspense. But stay cool.

Jimmy hung up the phone and coiled and uncoiled his fingers on the wheel, taking long, even breaths. He wanted another pop. Wanted one bad. It hadn't been long since his last, but he thought maybe long enough. He wouldn't have time once they got to Tony's house, but maybe he could pull it off driving. He could put it in his neck. He'd done that before. And he could see his bulging jugular standing out under the tight skin of his throat.

He had a pop ready to go in his console and he fished it out, being sure to keep the car even on the road. The monkey was steadily there, encouraging him, pushing him, taunting him.

The prick of the needle was a sexual delight, and the electric flood in his veins orgasmic. Goose-flesh mounded, and he dropped the needle to the floorboard.

*Keep it cool,* Jimmy thought.

*"That's right,"* the demon monkey chittered in his ear. In his mind. *"Keep it cool."*

Jimmy thought he could do that. After all, what was cooler than ice?

# Chapter 15

Tony hissed a curse as he tapped the end call icon on his phone. Jantz still wasn't answering his calls. He'd left multiple messages over the past several days, but it wasn't until today that it really started worrying him. Because today was the day Tony had gotten the money, and he and Jantz were supposed to meet up about it. Go over how to invest it. Small deposits, here and there, spread out over time. Nothing to raise a red flag about.

But the son of a bitch wasn't answering his damned phone.

Tony cursed again, wondering what to do. Savage would be turning into a problem soon, even with Tony's leverage over him. The man was a cunt, but he wasn't a stupid cunt. If Tony didn't get out of here, and soon, a whole lot of FUBAR would be coming down on him in no time.

He dropped onto his couch and clicked on the television. It was tuned to an old Frasier episode, and he immediately changed the channel. He hated high-brow comedy. And the snots on this show were nothing but a pair of sissy little faggots pretending to like women. Only their old man was worth watching, but they made him into half a fucking fairy too a great deal of the time. What the fuck was funny about rich snobs who enjoyed the opera?

No, he couldn't abide that. And anyway, he wasn't in the mood for comedy, high-brow or not. He didn't know just what he *was* in the mood for, but it wasn't that.

He stopped on the Dallas affiliate for NBC News. There was a report about a home invasion in Big D. Tony liked hearing about home invasions. Home invasions were interesting. They had mystique and pizazz. Something Tony thought he might like to try some day on some cunts. The thought made his dick hard. Was there anything more totally demoralizing and debilitating than a person at the mercy of a real man who'd come into their home?

Home invasions were a thing Tony thought he could get into. They had—

His thoughts stopped cold when he read the highlight on the bottom of the screen and his bowels felt like they were turning to water. Then he recognized the house exterior on the screen behind the reporter, a sexy little blond thing whose face and tits he'd normally like to imagine spraying his swimmers over, but not now. Not with the realization of what he was seeing unfold.

It was Jantz's house. Tony couldn't believe his eyes, and his ears were no better. The reporter was talking about a decorated Dallas detective whose home had been invaded and whose entire family had been slain. There were reports of mutilation, of torture.

"Oh, my fucking God," Tony mumbled to the empty house, his thickening dick withering.

He clicked off the TV. It was time to go. Tony knew better than to try and assume this was a random coincidence. He knew who they'd stolen from. Jantz and him had gone over it all in detail. Gone over how to fuck the others out of the whole deal, and not have their prints or presence anywhere near the investigation. It was supposed to be perfect. Had Jantz fucked up? And if so, how?

But that didn't really matter now. What mattered was getting the fuck out, and fast.

He snatched his holster, which held his Glock, off the kitchen counter and grabbed the keys to his car. Then he was heading for the garage, picking up the bags of cash on the way and dropping his pistol into one of them. Then he was in his garage, tossing the bags into the trunk, about to slam the lid closed.

*Where the hell am I gonna go?* he thought. *Jantz is dead. He was the one with the plan. What the hell am I going to do?*

That would just have to wait. He had to go *somewhere.* Anywhere was better than here, where he was predictable and findable. He'd hole up somewhere and work it out then.

He slammed the lid and slid into his car. He punched the button on his garage door remote and the door behind him began to lift noisily into the air. He shut his door. Threw the car into reverse. Began to back out.

Then a pair of headlights ramped up into his driveway, directly behind him, blocking his exit.

"God-damnit!" he hissed as he shifted back to drive and returned his car to the garage.

*Who the hell is this?*

He killed the engine and stepped out. He reached for his pistol, and cold fear stole over him as he realized he'd left it in the bag. The bag was in the trunk. And for all he knew the car in the driveway was the guy they'd stolen from, come to collect his due.

A chill forced him to shudder against his will as the door to the other car opened. He stood there, frozen in the wash of the headlamps, as a dark figure emerged. Then another pair of headlights came up to the curb next to his driveway and stopped.

*I'm dead,* he thought simply and immediately. *I'm fucking dead. They caught me. The cunt found me.*

"Where do you think you're going?" a voice said to him. It was coming from the figure who'd stepped out of the first car.

Behind them, the second car's lights blinked off and someone climbed out. Tony could hardly see past the headlights. Little more than shadows. His hand came up to shield his eyes.

"W-who's there?" Tony questioned, his voice betraying him.

A second later, the lights clicked off and he dropped his hand. The first figure was stepping into the garage, a second was getting out of the passenger side, and the third was coming up the driveway.

Then he saw it was Savage.

A great whoosh exhaled from Tony then. A pent-up wind of terror, blowing away all at once. He hadn't been aware he was holding his breath until it happened.

It was Savage, his bitch, and the junkie. A problem, to be sure, but one he should have no problem dealing with.

And deal with it he would.

# Chapter 16

John stared at Tony for a moment. The man was clearly recovering from a scare, and John liked that he'd been able to give that to him. Liked it quite a lot. It felt good for once to be on the delivering end of such an emotion with the motherfucker, and he relished it for a moment.

Then he repeated his question.

"Where do you think you're going?"

Jenny was beside him now, and Jimmy came into the garage a moment later. Immediately, Jimmy's nervous energy seemed to fill the air like a thick fog. From the corner of his eyes, John could see he was clawing at his arms, his head twitching, muffled curses hissing through his locked teeth. His head kept turning ever so slightly, and he was mumbling something to no one under his breath between the curses.

"Get the fuck out of here, Savage," Tony said, then looked to the others. "All of you."

"You don't check your voicemail, do you?" John asked, ignoring his demand. "I've been trying to reach you."

"I don't answer to you, cunt," Tony said with disgust.

"Larry's dead," John said flatly, dispensing with any more build up.

This seemed to startle Tony. His eyes widened, then narrowed and dropped to the floor in thought.

"Jesus," Tony whispered. "Two already."

This pricked John's ears. His eyes narrowed and he turned an ear towards Tony just slightly as he took another step forward.

"What do you mean *two*?" John asked.

Tony shook his head, seeming to clear it, then looked up again and met John's gaze.

"Fuck you!" Jimmy suddenly hissed over his shoulder and caught them all off guard. All eyes were now on him. He clawed at his arm and at his throat. He twisted his head around, bones cracking, his teeth bared in an enraged snarl.

But he didn't seem to notice any of them staring at him in wonderment. He merely kept on with his clawing and muffled murmurs, seemingly oblivious to the rest of them.

Letting it go once more without confrontation, John strode to the garage door button and pressed it. The door came down, locking them all inside, the others finally averting their concerned gaze from the unravelling Jimmy. Then John put a hand on Jimmy's shoulder, squeezed it, and gave him a nod. Jimmy's eyes twitched and his head jerked. He was breathing too fast and he was nearly soaked through with sweat.

*This is not the time!* John thought bitterly, but went back to the business at hand and approached Tony.

"What do you mean two?" he repeated when he stood before Tony once more.

Tony's face gnarled in condescension, but John could detect fear in his eyes. You could always see a person's real feelings, their emotions. It was in their eyes. The eyes were incapable of deception.

"Jantz," Tony said.

The name meant nothing to John.

"Who?"

"Jantz," Tony repeated, shaking his head and looking to a space on the floor between them. "My guy in DPD. The one who told me about the job."

John nodded. "He's dead too?"

Now it was Tony's turn to nod.

"I-I just saw it on the news," Tony explained. "Goddamn home invasion. Killed his whole family. Mutilation. The whole bit."

John's breath caught in his throat. Jimmy had told him what he had seen at Larry's. Any fleeting hope of coincidence was gone now. Whoever they had stolen from was coming for them, and coming hard.

"We need to get the money and get out of here," John said. "Where is it?"

Tony didn't answer, but his eyes glanced briefly at the trunk of his car and then back to John. To John it seemed involuntary.

"Your trunk?" John asked.

Tony said nothing, but his expression spoke volumes. A sigh escaped him, ever so slightly, and the hint of a snarl threatening to form on his face, though he was suppressing it. But it was too late. John had seen it.

It all fell into place for John then. Tony, grabbing the money that morning with a speech about cleaning it. Tony, who'd set the job up in the first place with this Jantz character. Tony, who had been about to take off with all of it.

Suddenly, the Beretta was in John's hand, wavering as he aimed it at Tony. He didn't remember pulling it from the small of his back, but it was out, and his finger was in the trigger guard.

"Time to start telling the truth for once, motherfucker," John said in a quiet tone.

Behind him, Jenny's breath caught audibly.

"Oh, baby, no," she sobbed. He could hear her hand clamp over her mouth.

"It's all good, honey," John said over his shoulder, never taking his eyes off Tony. "This is under control."

But it wasn't. He knew it, she knew it, they all knew it. The last thing any part of this resembled was control.

He continued in on Tony.

"Who the fuck did we steal from?" John asked, his voice nearly trembling. "What the fuck did you get us into?"

Tony glared back at him, his mouth a grimace, his eyes swimming with fear and rage in equal measure.

"I told you before, Savage, this guy got into a tangle at a bar and—"

"No!" John screamed, cutting him off. "No more bullshit, Tony! Tell us the truth. Larry's dead! His whole family is dead! His *kid* is dead, god-damn you! Your friend is dead. His family too. You owe it to them, you owe it to the rest of us! Now tell me the fucking truth, and if you lie again, so help me, I will *end* you!"

The words had come out like a flamethrower. John's tongue was hot, and he could tell the words had burned Tony as well. His face was shed of all contempt, now showing only dread. He exhaled.

"It was..." Tony started, then stopped a moment. He was visibly trembling. "Jantz, he, well he knew about this guy. A guy for hire. You know, like a cleaner. A problem solver."

"You mean a fucking hitman?" Jenny cut in then, still sobbing softly.

Tony shrugged. "You could call it that, I guess, yeah. Jantz was investigating this killing. Some nigger found in a warehouse. Fucking spike in his kneecap. Bad scene. But Jantz, he found something. It wasn't much, so he didn't clue in his partner. Wanted to follow it up, see if it led anywhere first."

John motioned with the gun for him to hurry up.

"Get to it, Tony," he growled.

Tony nodded again, his throat clicking as he swallowed.

"Anyway, he found this guy. Nice neighborhood, no criminal record, nothing. The guy's a ghost. Jantz starts checking into the guy some more, looks up his bank accounts, investments, stuff like that."

"And?"

"And the guy didn't have very much. Not on paper, anyways. Guys like this, they make good money. Lots of it. Lots of risk involved, lots of reward. But he wasn't living large. He was just living. So Jantz figured the guy must be stashing it away. Like disappearing money, in case something came down on him all at once. He wouldn't keep that in a bank account or safe deposit box. He'd keep it close. And that's how it started."

His words hung in the air.

Behind them, Jimmy was clicking his teeth together, over and over again, as though biting at the air. Jenny was still sobbing. John was overcome with anger.

"You got us involved in robbing a hitman, and thought you were keeping yourselves clean in the process? Sending me and Jimmy and Larry in there while you and Jantz provided security?"

Tony's smug smile returned, in spite of his obvious fear.

"You're such a cunt, Savage, you know that? Don't you stand here and get all sanctimonious on me, asshole. You were plenty willing for a cut of that score. And get the god-damn gun out of my face."

John didn't.

Instead, he went on.

"You're right, I was willing. But if I'd known the truth about who we were taking it from, I would have walked. We all would have."

Tony's lips twitched and a smile nearly formed. Then he had control of it and the scowl returned. John's eyes narrowed at this.

"And you knew that, didn't you?" John asked, almost rhetorically. "You knew we'd never go for it, that's why you made up the bullshit story about the guy in the bar."

"Fucking, fucker!" Jimmy hissed behind them.

John started to turn, but as he did, Tony took a step towards him, and John raised the gun and leveled it on him again.

"Don't you fucking move!"

Tony stopped and took a step back.

"And what were you doing when we got here, Tony?" John asked. "Taking the money and hauling ass?"

John heard a crunching sound behind him in Jimmy's direction. He huffed a sigh, knowing he was popping another pill.

"Fuck you, Savage," Tony hissed, his face a contorted mess, his eyes swimming with terror. "Fuck you and your junkie pal and your bitch, and—"

John cocked the hammer of his Beretta.

"You watch your mouth, motherfucker!"

"You don't have the balls, Savage!" Tony raged, his arms waving about wildly. "You're a cunt! You're all cunts! This was the biggest score you've ever seen, and you got to be in on it because of *me*! Because *I* didn't turn you in when you wasted that fuck on Pine Street! You wouldn't have *anything* without me, and you call *me* the motherfucker? That's a gas, Savage!"

"Shut up!" John barked. "You used us! You were going to take the money and run. What, were you just waiting on Jantz until you found out he was dead, is that it?"

"Fuck you," Tony spat. "Go on, pull that trigger, I dare you! I *double*-dare you, motherfucker!"

"Stop pushing me."

"Baby, please don't—" Jenny started.

"Yeah Savage, listen to your lady there like a good little pussy!" Tony mocked.

Jimmy began screaming like a maniac behind them, but no one seemed to notice. All of John's focus was on the dirty piece of shit before him.

"Baby, please!" Jenny pleaded over the din of Jimmy's roar.

"God-damn you, Tony!" John hissed through clenched teeth. Sweat stood out on his brow and the barrel wavered.

"Yeah, god-damn me, god-damn you, god-damn all of you!" Tony threw back. "Now listen to your bitch and drop the—"

Tony's face imploded.

A red and gray shower blossomed from the back of Tony's head as it jerked back and he began to fall. Someone, somewhere, was screaming. But John could barely hear it over the ringing in his ears. He hadn't even heard the shot. Smoke rose from the barrel of his gun and he was faintly aware of the aftershock in his hand from the soft recoil of the gun.

He turned. Everything was moving in slow motion. The ringing was still covering all other sound, but he could see Jenny there, her eyes saucers, hands clenched over her mouth. Jimmy was behind her, screaming at the wall at nothing. At absolutely nothing.

And the revolver was in his hand.

The ringing subsided enough that he heard the soft thump as Tony's body collapsed to the floor of the garage. He couldn't take his eyes off of Jimmy. John pulled Jenny against him. She was shaking and sobbing, her back rising and falling as she hitched breath.

"Calm down, baby," he whispered to her, but she didn't. She continued on, a total breakdown of control.

Jimmy stopped screaming at the wall, and just stared at it. The hand holding the revolver shook and twitched and jerked. His finger was on the trigger, and John wondered how it hadn't gone off yet.

"Jimmy, what the fuck, man?" John hollered over Jenny's sobs. "Snap out of it! We have to get the money and get out of here!"

Jimmy turned to him, his eyes nearly bulging out of their sockets, that malicious abortion of a smile on his lips—the same one he'd seen as they'd left his apartment—making a triumphant comeback.

*Oh, my God,* John thought. *He's completely lost it.*

"Johnny," Jimmy said, his voice too high and strained, "you're an asshole. You're all assholes. And you're not fucking me out of my share!"

John was flabbergasted. "What the hell are you talking about? Tony was trying to cut us out, not me!"

Jenny's cries had subsided, and now she turned around, her back still against John's chest, and faced Jimmy. John could feel her body tense as she saw the gun in his hand and the expression on his face.

"Jimmy, baby, what are you doing?" She asked as sweetly as she could, the last remnants of sobs dusting her voice, her hands out before her in a calming gesture. "You're family to us!"

"I smell bullshit!" Jimmy said in a mocking, sing-song voice. "I'm no dairyman, but I know it when I smell it!"

John realized Jimmy was completely mad. Whether it was the drugs or the stress of seeing Larry's family the way he had, he wasn't sure. It was probably both. But he'd clearly had a complete psychotic break. His view of reality was completely skewed now.

And he had a fucking gun.

"Jimmy," John said as soft and even as he could manage, "Put the gun down. No one's cutting you out. No one's doing anything like that."

Then Jimmy broke in a high-pitched cackle of laughter. It was like a terrible clown's laugh, if that clown were a shape-shifting, cosmic monster living in the sewers under a small town in Maine.

It sent chills down John's spine. He felt gooseflesh rise on Jenny's arms.

"Oh-ho," Jimmy said through his laughter, "somebody's getting cut out, but it ain't fucking me!"

The laughter returned in full force as Jimmy raised the revolver. John's breath caught and he was aware of his own gun coming up, preparing to fire on his friend, his *brother*, the one he'd loved and looked out for. The one he'd have done anything in the world for.

The one he'd murdered for.

But he wasn't fast enough. There was another roar of gunfire and Jenny leaned into John hard and sudden. There was a terrible pain in the left side of John's torso and his gun clattered to the floor to his side. Then he was falling, the pain swelling to a crescendo as he went down. And Jenny was falling too, almost right on top of him.

John's head was spinning. He was on the ground now, pain pulsating through his side, and Jimmy was scrambling like a madman to Tony's car. John coughed, then winced against an explosion of exquisite pain.

The garage door was going up a moment later and Jimmy was sprinting out. John lolled his head to the side and saw Jimmy jumping into the Subaru, still chittering laughter the whole time.

John slid out from under Jenny as his own car sped away behind him. He shook his head to clear it, then looked down to his side where the pain was coming from.

There was a tear in his shirt and a little bit of blood, but upon closer inspection, he realized he'd only been grazed. It was close, but ultimately only superficial. He would be fine.

"Jenny, baby," he said, still staring at his wound and wincing. "He grazed me, looks like. But I'll be fine I thi—"

He stopped midsentence. He was raising his eyes from his wound to her face as he'd been talking, and what he saw drove an icicle into his bowels.

Her lips were trying to move, and her eyes were darting around at the ceiling. Blood dribbled from her mouth, and her left breast was wounded badly. Blood pumped from it and her white shirt blossomed with scarlet petals which seemed to grow and spread like a vine.

John's eyes stung at once, horror and confusion filling them. His breath came in gasps and seemed to pause as though he'd forgotten how to breathe for several seconds.

"Johnny, I..." she whispered through blood-soaked lips.

He pulled her quickly into his arms, embracing her. He put his hand over the wound on her chest, pressing hard.

"Jenny?" his voice came out in a strange tenor. "Jenny, baby, it's gonna be okay! I'm—I'm g-gonna get...get you..."

He broke into full sobs then. Uncontrollable waves of lamentation poured from him as he looked into her eyes, which he could see were dimming even now.

Somewhere outside, a universe away, the sound of his Subaru's tires squealing flowed into John's ears, though it hardly registered with him. Jimmy was speeding away. He was running away from shooting Jenny, the sweet, precious, loving woman who'd always treated Jimmy like family. But still he'd shot her. And now she was choking on her own blood in John's arms.

John pushed thoughts of Jimmy aside for the moment and focused on her eyes. He was fumbling his phone out, intending to call 9-1-1, and he cursed when he couldn't get the screen to unlock.

Jenny coughed, and blood speckled his face. He looked to her, forgetting his contrary phone. She was looking into his eyes, her mouth working as if trying to say something.

"Shh-shh," he said, brushing the side of her face with the backs of his fingers. "Just hang in there, baby, I'm gonna call the ambulance."

He reached once more for his phone, and again began fumbling with it. This time he got the screen to unlock and he quickly thumbed the phone icon. But before he could pull up the dial-pad and call for help, her hand reached up and cupped his face. He turned to her, and looked into her ever-widening eyes.

Jenny tried a final time working her mouth, and this time was able to get out what she'd been trying to say. As John heard the three little words, his blood ran cold and his skin chilled, gooseflesh rising on every part of his body. He knew he could not be hearing this, could not be *seeing* this, but there it was. Right before him in horrifying clarity.

*"I love you."*

Blood flowed in a stream from the corner of her mouth as the dimming light in her eyes was snuffed out completely and she went limp in his arms.

He stared at her in disbelief for what seemed an eternity. His eyes stung. His heart was exploding in his chest. He shivered on the floor of the garage between the motherfucker cop who'd tried to screw them all and the love of his life, limp in his arms. The pain in his side was a distant itch.

How could he have gotten here? How could this have happened when only a short while ago they were at their apartment, together? And how could Jimmy have turned on them like this?

But how this all happened was irrelevant, he knew. The how of it all dissolved away into insignificant detritus as he clutched Jenny's limp body in his arms. Pain welled in his heart, a physical thing, punctuated with his sobs.

How it all happened didn't matter.

What he was going to do about it was his focus now. Deep rage began to writhe through him, his limbs shook and his muscles vibrated. His jaw locked and his mouth drew tight.

*I'll kill you, Jimmy Hanson!* he thought as his teeth began to bare in a snarl. *I'll end you!*

He gently kissed Jenny's bloody face, and lay her on the floor of the garage. He would be back for her when his business was done with Jimmy. He would do right by her. The way she deserved. He would not leave her here to rot next to Tony and be discovered by the neighbors inspecting the smell.

He would not allow that.

"I love you," he whispered, dragging himself to his feet.

As he steadied himself, he looked down to his lover, so still now. He was horrified to find the pain was fleeting, replaced now with a black rage. Something else Jimmy had done in the blink of an eye. He couldn't even mourn Jenny for his all-consuming rage, and he realized he hated Jimmy with everything inside of him. Jimmy had been like his brother, but now he hated him. Hate was a bitter flavor, and John realized he liked the taste of it.

*I'll fix you, motherfucker,* he thought as a wild grin split his features.

He reached to the ground and picked up his Beretta. He hefted the weight in his hand a moment, then cocked the hammer.

*I'll fix you good!*

He ran to Tony's car—a hopped-up Mustang—and jumped in. The keys were still in it and the engine roared to life. He pushed back a fresh wave of grief for Jenny before they stole over him completely and instead focused on the festering, pus-filled hate for Jimmy at his center. There would be time to mourn later. But not now. Right now, he had business to attend to.

Jimmy Hanson had a debt to pay and John Savage had the fucking bill.

# Chapter 17

John was panting as he roared onto the street, his eyes darting around to see if anyone was watching him. Panic, fury, and a damning sense of dread, of *doom,* in the pit of his stomach were causing his head to spin.

*Did anyone hear the shots?*

He didn't know. Hell, he *couldn't* know. Not for sure. Not yet, anyway. His ears still rung faintly from the deafening booms in the garage.

He dropped the accelerator to the floor and he was off like lightning. There were no signs of alarm anywhere as he sped away, and that was good. The .38 Special wasn't the loudest of weapons, but the 9mm Parabellum *was* loud. And any way you cut it, a gunshot is never quiet.

He swerved onto Main, glancing in his rearview mirror to look at Tony's house once more, where his now-dead lover lay in a pool of her own blood, lifeless. Tears ripped through his ducts and spilled over his cheeks. The rage swelled fresh and new again, a delicious balm. He floored the accelerator, channeling his pain and anguish into raw horsepower. The Mustang's tires barked, then gripped the pavement and launched him forward even faster.

*God-damn you, Jimmy!* his mind screamed. *Why? After everything I've done for you, why? You motherfu—*

He jerked the wheel to the right, heading down a small street, and brushed tears and snot from his face with the sleeve of his jacket. He winced as the graze wound on the side of his torso protested, but he pushed the pain away. Rage was overriding his other emotions now, and he saw ahead exactly what he'd expected to see, though it still cut off all other thoughts.

The tail-lights of his Subaru—of *Jenny's* Subaru—dead ahead.

"You're gonna pay for this, Jimmy!" he screamed into the cab of Tony's car. "You're gonna p—"

The car hit a pothole he hadn't noticed and he felt the undercarriage scrape as sparks flung out in all directions from the car. The car swerved a bit, but he got it back under control quickly and pushed the accelerator down again. The distance was closing quickly, and John's vision narrowed to a pinpoint directly on the back of the Subaru.

Larry was dead. Someone had found him and was now coming for the rest of them. This should have drawn them together. To watch each other's backs. They always had before. But instead, Tony-*that motherfucker*-had tried to take off with everything. Why in hell had they ever agreed to any of this? Why hadn't he just taken the asshole down with him that night when he'd pulled Jimmy out of the crack house? He'd have been better off. They'd all have been better off. And Jenny would...would be...

*Alive.*

That's what she would be. He would be in jail, maybe on death row, but she would be *alive*, god-damnit, and this was all his fault. And Jimmy's fault, that fucker. God, how had this all happened? What had turned Jimmy so suddenly?

He decided it didn't matter. What had happened had happened. It was done. Whether it was the drugs or a mental break, or both, it didn't matter. All that mattered now was to finish his business with Jimmy and get out. He thought of Jenny's body, lying next to the asshole cop who'd set all of this in motion. No, he wouldn't leave her there. *Couldn't* leave her there. He'd find a way to get her out of there and he'd bury her himself. Somewhere only he would know about. Some place special.

The engine roared as he sped faster.

# Chapter 18

Spears was agitated. His jaw was tight, and his furrowed brow brimmed with a light film of sweat. The Jimmy Hanson fellow *had* to show up soon. He just had to. They were spinning their wheels and time was wasting. Every second they were out there and his money wasn't found was tantamount to total failure. Total loss.

Something he could not allow.

Yet, here he sat. An empty house, save for Vic and Paul. Well, and the dead mongrel in the hallway, let's not forget about the mutt. His associates had torn the place apart, top to bottom, looking for the money. He'd dug around some himself, but mostly he'd bristled. Feeling his anger clench him tighter and tighter, starting at the pit of his stomach and rising like acid into his esophagus. He'd had to focus on controlling his breathing, finally. It was coming in rasps and heaves as he envisioned using the spikes on these dumb fucks. Oh, he'd find his money, friends and neighbors, you could count on that. But he'd relish every pounding blow of the hammer and every wet sob of agony. It would be music. Something he could shake a god-damned leg to. And he'd really do a number on the bitch. It would be good to see the Savage fuck squirm as he drove a spike into her fucking cunt. Oh, that would be a gas.

He snapped out of his fantasy and realized his dick was hard.

This made him smile, though it was already beginning to whither. They'd found nothing so far. Not a single red cent. And his fantasies of medieval torture on the cock-sucking fools who'd stolen from him were only doing so much to calm his nerves. He needed blood.

The real thing.

And he meant to drink it from their fucking boots.

But he'd begun to think perhaps the money wasn't here at all. Could be at the cop's place, he supposed. That seemed like the most logical place to stash it. Or it could be in the Savage man's apartment. In fact, the more he poured over the whole thing, the more he was convinced it *must* be at one of the other two places. Because it sure as shit wasn't here.

*Maybe they already took off with it,* he thought and grimaced.

It was possible, he supposed. But not likely. People like these wouldn't leave the dog behind, the one now rotting in the hallway. They'd come for it.

*Maybe only one of them took the money and left. What about that?*

Spears cursed himself under his breath. He'd elected to search here first because based on the blood-soaked information he'd ripped out of Larry Horowitz, Jimmy was the weakest link in the chain. He hadn't really thought the money would be here, but he was sure he could crack Hanson the easiest and he would lead them straight to it. But his plan hadn't panned out.

*Fucking amateur,* Spears thought as he rubbed a hand over his frustrated face. *You acted like a fucking amateur. You're too close to this.*

That was the hell of it.

The jobs he worked for his myriad clients were cold things. He had no attachment to them. No vested interest. Just a job. A paycheck. Nothing more.

But this was *his* money.

*His* stash.

His getaway funds, should he ever need to disappear at a moment's notice. Vanishing money. Something that needed to be on hand, close by. Something he could put his hands on in a snap and slip away. He had to have it back. He *needed* the money.

And it was clouding his judgment.

He sighed loudly and dropped himself on the couch in the living room. It squeaked as he dropped in. And continued dropping. It was as if the thing had no supports at all inside it and he just kept going, almost falling into it. His hands shot out involuntarily to steady himself, to catch himself on the cushions, but they began to sink as well. His startled eyes widened and his feet slipped out from beneath him as though in parody of his situation. Wires groaned and wood creaked and *he was still falling*!

"Stupid, fucking—" he began and then barked a short howl of pain as something beneath him poked or pinched his ass—he didn't know which—and he arched his back trying to get free of the man-eating couch monster before it swallowed him whole.

His arms were flailing now, clawing at the front of the couch, grasping for purchase. Sweat stung his eyes as his feet kicked before him helplessly. He reached forward, grunting and wheezing breaths hissing through his clenched teeth.

His hand clasped the front support-*what a fucking joke*-and his fingers gripped it tightly. He began to heave himself forward, up and out of the bottomless couch. Vic came in then, and his expression immediately turned to one of surprise and *(God help him if he laughs)* bemusement.

"The fuck, boss?" he said, obviously stifling a laugh as he crossed the room and reached for Spears's hand. Spears meant to rip the man's trachea out if he heard so much as a single chirp of laughter.

"Son of a bitch," Spears muttered under his breath as Vic pulled him to his feet.

Spears began shaking his arms out and brushing himself off, his face red and flushed.

"What hap—"

Spears's hand shot out and pinched Vic's cheeks together into comical fish mouth.

"Not a fucking word," he rasped.

Vic's eyes were wide and he nodded furiously, his hands going up in surrender. Spears released him and turned to the couch, spat on it, then kicked it with the heel of his shoe. He took a deep breath and turned to Vic to say something.

But before he could get a word out, there came a crashing sound from just up the road. Metal crunching and glass shattering and tires squealing. A woman screamed.

Spears and Vic scrambled to the window and jerked the shade back. Paul was hustling into the room behind them then.

"The fuck?" Paul said, his breaths coming in heaves.

Spears's eyes were glued to the scene outside, his face a picture of bemused wonder.

About fifty yards down the street there was a two way stop intersection. The road Jimmy Hanson's house was on was required to stop, while the intersecting road was unyielding. Just this side of the intersection were three mangled cars. Glass littered the intersection, and the shards glinted in the light of the streetlamp. Smoke rose from the rear car in ghostly tendrils.

It appeared the car in the middle had smashed into the other two as it drove on the unyielding road, but Spears couldn't be sure. Whatever had happened, it was bad. He could see blood and the faint movement of silhouettes in the front and rear car, though none he could make out in the middle one. That was when he noticed the woman's scream he'd heard only a moment ago had ceased. Just the one cry, then nothing.

The car closest to him was only clipped in the back, Spears noticed now. Vic and Paul had joined him at the window at some point, and their eyes matched his own in wonderment and surprise, their jaws hanging open stupidly.

For several moments, the cars just sat there unmoving, save for the shadows within. But then, to his astonishment, the closest car started to pull away. The rear of the car was badly twisted, and the car seemed to tremble as it rambled down the street, but it was moving. Picking up speed.

"I'll be damned," Vic said.

The car was moving faster and faster from the wreck. Spears shifted his gaze back to the sight of the wreck and saw two things: a body lying on the sidewalk surrounded with what must have been an explosion of blood—perhaps ejected from the middle car—and a man climbing out of the farthest car. The man was hobbling, or limping, favoring his right leg a great deal. And Spears could just make out something in the man's hand. Spears squinted, trying to discern what it was, but it was too dark.

"This is fucked," Paul said. "Now we're gonna have damn police all over the place!"

Spears nodded. This *was* fucked. And bad. Like dry and in the ass bad. They needed to—

The limping man lifted the object in his hand towards the battered car which was speeding away. There was a small flash of light followed closely by a very loud *BANG!*

*A gun.*

This was *not* good. If the wreck weren't bad enough, now these redneck assholes were shooting at each other! Cops would be showing up soon. A multiple car accident leading into a shooting tended to draw their attention.

*This is bad, Bad, BAD!*

When the shot rang out, glass shattered in the rear windshield of the fleeing vehicle. Spears had time to witness a misting of red inside the car—again, illuminated by another streetlight—and the car swerved.

Spears's breath caught in his throat. The car had swerved, and it was continuing to swerve right towards them. The trajectory was unmistakable. The car was bouncing up over the curb, the roaring whine of the engine audible to them now, and seemed to be continuing to gain speed. Sparks sprayed out from beneath the car as it bounced and the head of the silhouette inside lolled about.

The car was about to crash into the window where they stood.

They all turned as if on cue and dived away from the window. A second later, perhaps less, the wall behind them exploded. Glass and drywall were flying all around them, raining down on them as the air whooshed out of their chests. They had just gotten clear before the car came through, but they were now covered in powder from the drywall and flakes of glass and siding and only God knew what were peppered all over them.

Spears heaved in a breath, forcing his lungs to resume normal operations, and pushed himself off the floor. He winced as he did this, as he felt a painful bruise beneath his left arm where his gun rested in its holster. Then he looked to the car.

He saw a man sitting behind the wheel, his face was bloody and cut, his eyes glazed and unaware. There was a nasty wound in his shoulder and he was trembling. Then the man began muttering. Insane ravings from the sound of it. Spears's face was a mural of heightened awareness and dumbfounded astonishment.

"Where'd you go, you fucking chimp?!" the man was raving. "Gotta get our god-damn dog."

*Dog,* Spears thought, understanding spilling over his face. *Is this the junk—*

The sound of the other man from the wreck jerked Spears's attention back to the here and now. He could hear the man yelling, almost screaming something. And he was getting closer, limping or not. The screaming was unintelligible at first, but as he pulled his pistol free of its holster and strained to hear, he finally made out what the man was saying.

And his suspicions of who the man in the car before him was were confirmed.

"JIMMY!"

"Get out there," Spears whispered to Vic and Paul, who were already moving. "It's them."

Spears pulled his pistol as Jimmy thrust the door to the mangled car open and stepped into the yard.

# Chapter 19

The lights in Jimmy's rearview mirror were growing larger and brighter as he sped towards his house. The fucking chimp was also there, its matted, hairy head framed in silhouette.

It laughed. An unending stream high-pitched, manic chatter.

*Get Roscoe and get the fuck out,* he thought behind his wide-stretched, crazy eyes.

He heard the roar of an engine behind him. A big one. V8, and hopped-up from the sound of it. The exhaust was screaming a bellowing belch of raw horsepower, utterly covering the whine of the Subaru's turbo.

"Is that you, Johnny?" he said, glancing into the rearview again. The monkey continued its chatter, its trebly cackles piercing through the bass of the roaring engine coming up on them.

Jimmy's eyes whipped back to the road in front of him. He could feel the skin stretched tight around them and realized his jaw was clamped tight. He was soaring, more ice in his system than he'd ever had before, and the effect was sheer madness.

He loved it.

Then he noticed the stop sign rushing up to the right of the road, much too fast for him to try and stop, but his foot reacted on instinct and pressed the brake.

The roar of the powerful engine behind him reached a crescendo and then he was lurching forward as the car behind him smashed into the trunk of the Subaru with a monumental force. Metal sang, terribly off-key, the sound of tires squealing leaped into the night like a shrieking demon.

Still, the monkey laughed. Jimmy thought if it didn't quit, he might go mad. He had a faint understanding that he was perhaps already mad, he was on the verge of going into an abyss of insanity which knew no bottom, a pit leading to hell itself.

The car lurched upward from the rear as the Mustang smashed the Subaru, its engine roaring, and Jimmy's nose smashed into the steering wheel. He felt rather than heard the cartilage shred, and warm fluid flooded down his face and shirt.

*"Fuck!"*

There was no doubt about it. It was Johnny, in full-on vengeance mode, coming for him. Jimmy had just put a bullet through one of Jenny's beautiful big titties, and he should have put one in Johnny too. He'd thought there was no need, thought the bullet had gotten them both from the way Johnny had gone down with her, but no. No, he was listening to the fucking demon monkey, chattering in his ear to *get the money, get the money, get the fucking money and go, go, GO!*

Jimmy had no time for this, and he was no match for Johnny. He knew it. But here Johnny was, live and in technicolor, smashing into the rear of his own car and driving it through the intersection.

And now there were headlights coming from his left. He was lit up like a deer in the middle of the road. It was coming on fast. Too fast. They were going to drive right into the side of the car, probably obliterate him in the process, and the god-damned monkey was still laughing!

*"Oh, shit!"* he yelped as his eyes nearly popped from their sockets.

In another second, the third car would be smashing into him, crushing him, turning him into a pulpy gelatin, all just mere yards from his house, Roscoe, and escape.

He braced himself for the impact which would certainly bring his demise. He pinched his eyes shut and gripped the wheel tighter, feeling the slickness of his blood on it. He wanted to tell the monkey to shut up, but his breath locked tight in his lungs and he couldn't make a sound.

But then, his door was past the headlights. They were now more in line with the rear passenger door, and he started to believe he might just miss it altogether and it would take Johnny out instead of him. Maybe even give him the precious moments he desperately needed to get away and grab Roscoe and get gone.

He was just going to make it, by no more than the width of a hair, but by God he would—

But he didn't. Perhaps it was the dazed state of his head which had thrown off his perception of the trajectory, or maybe it was the ice raging through his system, or even that he'd just been overly hopeful, but whatever the reason, he had been wrong. The third car hit the tail-end of his, smashing the already crushed trunk into a crooked, warped ball. The trunk of the Subaru popped up in a mangled bobble. The third car also smashed into the front of the car Johnny was in with a loud crash, and smoke began filling the air. The back end of Jimmy's car swung around perhaps twenty degrees, but then stopped. His foot was still on the brake pedal, pushing it to the floor with all the force he had. His face throbbed and leaked blood in rivulets down both sides of his face. His breathing was coming in fast, hitching heaves. He tried getting it under control before he hyperventilated.

He looked in his side mirror, trying to assess the damage as best he could, and saw that it appeared he hadn't been hit all that bad by the third car. Not as bad as Johnny had been, that was for sure.

He turned his head to the other mirror, and from it he could see the body of a woman on the sidewalk, her head badly smashed, her legs and fingers twitching, one bulging eye staring out from a crushed and ruined socket.

She was dead. He was sure of it. Or at least she would be in short order. Blood was everywhere. She must have been ejected from the third car when they'd rushed out in front of her.

*Oh, shit, oh, fuck!*

*"Drive!"* the monkey roared, startling him from his horror.

His eyes snapped back to the rearview mirror and he could see the monkey, its fangs and black eyes an aberration, hissing like a rabid cat. He also saw the front of Tony's Mustang, badly smashed and tendrils of smoke billowing from the radiator. He could see the silhouette of his old friend stirring behind the wheel through the drifting haze. Smoke drifted and covered the outline, then parted again and the door to Johnny's car howled and bent on protesting hinges as it swung open.

Jimmy's foot finally released itself from the brake, and instinctively hit the accelerator of the Subaru, smashing it to the floor. It lurched forward, the chassis jarring and shivering as it moved, but by the grace of God or the luck of the devil, it *was* moving.

He sped down the street, wrestling with the wheel to keep it straight. The monkey continued to bark orders, telling him to *move, to go, take that mutt and his money and let's get another hit!*

He was very near to his house when he glanced once more into the rearview mirror and saw the flash.

The rear window exploded, and so did the monkey. It vanished like smoke in a high wind and drifted into the black. At the same time, he felt the breath knocked out of him and noticed a bullet hole appear in the front windshield, spider-webbing its surroundings. A fresh geyser of blood sprayed onto the spider-web, obliterating his vision. He gasped as operatic pain bellowed from his right shoulder, and that arm went limp. He began to swerve to the left, his good arm not responding properly, slipping on the slick blood all over the steering wheel.

He bounced over the curb, sparks flying, and had time to register that he was bounding into his own yard. There was his house, right in front of him, and in all the confusion and pain, he realized his foot was still smashed to the floor on the accelerator. His brain was trying to send the message to his foot to back the fuck off, stand on the brake, but it wasn't obeying. Shock had overridden the deity of his mind, and the rebel appendage was acting all on its own.

As his car rushed towards the large window—the one his couch sat in front of—he looked into his window, eyes bleary, and his breath caught in his throat.

There were three wide-eyed faces staring out at him. And was that...*the monkey?*

*What in the actual fu—*

Then he was crashing into his living room. His face once again made acquaintance with the steering wheel, his forehead this time, and he reeled back into the headrest, a jet of blood spritzing from his head. Glass exploded all around him, some of it imbedding itself in his face. An airbag exploded from the wheel in front of his face and drove his head back into the headrest again, the whiplash not unnoticed in his neck.

He sat there a moment, stunned, his heart thrumming in his chest at better than two-hundred beats per minute. Then the airbag was deflating out of his way. He looked past the bloody, cracked windshield and saw none of the faces he'd seen before. Certainly not the monkey. He winced, but not from pain this time. He was feeling no pain now, only shock and terror. He saw spots floating all around as he sat parked in his living room, and he willed them to clear.

"Where'd you go, you fucking chimp?" he asked and spat blood. "Gotta get our god-damn dog."

He wrenched the door open. It only opened part way, its full arc blocked by the side of his house, but it was enough. He hauled himself out with a wet grunt, absently pulling the .38 from his waist with his left hand.

He heard a scream from the road. A man's scream. And he recognized it. It was one he'd heard plenty of times before, especially when he'd been caught *'on that shit'* once again.

It was Johnny.

"JIMMY!"

He looked up and saw Johnny hobbling towards him, on the edge of his lawn now, clutching his side and dragging his left leg.

He also saw the gun in his hand.

Jimmy's malicious grin returned, the veins sticking out on his throat, and he raised his gun.

## Chapter 20

When he smashed into the rear of the Subaru, John's raging, grief-filled world went black. A moment later, his eyes snapped open and he watched in awed horror as a blonde woman on the curb in front of him, her head smashed to mush, gyrated limply in post-death convulsions. Her fingers twitched, and one foot jerked this way and that as her back rose and fell, dragging in its final breaths.

*Oh, Jesus.*

But he didn't have time for more remorse. Not now, not when he was so close to having his hands on the son-of-a-bitch in front of him. He dragged his gaze away from the dying woman and looked up to see Jimmy's car, the rear bashed in and crooked, but otherwise seemingly okay. He could see Jimmy turned around in the driver's seat, presumably staring at the dead woman who'd run into them.

John then glanced down at the front of the Mustang. It was a crumpled mess, the hood wadded up like a discarded scrap of paper, white smoke or steam billowing out in thin tendrils. It would not be running again.

He reached for the door, only now realizing his ears were ringing and humming, drowning out most other sound. He tried the door and was surprised to be able to open it, though with some difficulty. It groaned and squealed as it slung open on its skewed hinges, and he grunted as he threw his legs out.

As he prepared to stand, he noticed two things: his left leg was screaming at him to cease its use—right fucking now, as a matter of fact—and the Subaru Jimmy had stolen was starting to pull away. It was gaining speed, leaving in a hurry, albeit awkwardly.

He took a step towards Jimmy's fleeing car and his leg screamed once again, longer this time and with a bit more growl. He winced, putting his right forearm against the roof of his car for balance, and looked down to his leg. His upper thigh was bleeding profusely. A small, but ragged hole in it marked ground-zero of his pain, and his eyes narrowed in confused wonder.

*What the hell?*

Then he looked at the Beretta still in his hand—it had never left his hand since he'd snatched it from the floor back at Tony's house— and saw the barrel was smoking.

*Must've gone off in the wreck,* he thought, wincing once more as his leg reminded him of its discomfort.

*"Fuck it,"* he muttered in a huffing breath.

He snapped his head up, his eyes locking on the diminishing taillights of Jimmy's car, his face scowling. He limped and dragged his wounded leg and made his way around the woman's car, its own engine still wheezing a soft rumble.

Jimmy had made it about twenty-five yards or so, and was gaining speed all the time. John had no time to waste. He didn't have time to devise a plan. He didn't have time to find another car and give chase. They were not far from Jimmy's house now anyway, and he was going to give Jimmy, his brother, *that motherfucker*, the hard goodbye. Even if it was the last thing he did.

He raised the gun and fired. The rear window of the car exploded, small chunks of glass glittering in the light of the street lamps, and the car began to swerve, the tires squealing as it lolled back and forth across the width of the street. John dragged himself down the street, away from the steaming engines and the now still corpse of the woman who'd had the misfortune of following the rules of the road at the wrong time.

The Subaru began swerving harder, more acutely, and bounced up over the curb on the edge of Jimmy's yard, sparks flying and metal barking against the cement.

Then it wrecked into the side of Jimmy's house.

*Made it home, you son of a bitch*, John thought.

He limped faster and faster. His breathing was becoming more labored now, and the pain in his leg was reaching notes higher than the greatest of opera singers. The graze wound on his side was also making its presence known and his left hand clutched it as he tried to push away all the pain, focusing on the smoking heap of twisted and ruined Subaru jutting from the side of Jimmy's house all the way to just in front of the door, right about where the living room would be. John dug deep within himself, willing himself to keep going. He meant to get to Jimmy before the cocksucker quit breathing and give him a lead transfusion. Then one in the brain.

The guarantee.

Lights out.

Ticket punched.

His mouth wavered and grimaced, sweat trickling down his face now in thin streams, rage welling within him once more as a vision of Jenny, her breast bleeding, filled his mind again.

John Savage screamed.

"JIMMY!"

There was very little movement coming from the vehicle. John squinted his eyes, willing them to adjust to the darkness, trying to make out the outline of Jimmy's head above the seat. As they did, he could see a white bag, probably the airbag, drifting down and deflating as Jimmy appeared to...*talk?* He was looking over his shoulder again, talking to no one.

The trunk of the Subaru was up now, its interior light amazingly on and working, lighting the bags within. Other lights were coming on in houses all over the street now. The wreck and gunshot had no doubt caught people's attention, but that was no matter. John gave only a singular shit now, and it was putting Jimmy down like the rabid dog he'd become. He was beginning to think he may be on his last leg anyway, no pun intended. Blood was pouring from his wound at a rate he wouldn't have thought possible. The pain was exquisite, so dazzling that he was now becoming dizzy. Colorful dots and dark clouds began to fill his vision.

*Got the artery,* he thought to himself. *I shot myself in the goddamn artery.*

He shook his head, fighting off the pain and dizziness and spots. His vision cleared for a moment, and he could finally make out the back of Jimmy's head in the car. It was shaking back and forth, rising up.

John was getting closer, perhaps twenty yards away now. He stepped over the curb, no small feat as his leg, now roaring with white-hot agony, began threatening to buckle. He straightened it and continued his hobbling drag towards the rear of the car stuck in the side of the house.

He could hear the first sirens breaking in the distance. As he heard this, the door to the Subaru squealed open, a howling scream of metal, and Jimmy hauled himself out. His shoulder was bleeding and his face was an apocalyptic ruin of ripped flesh and smashed cartilage.

The sirens grew louder. He had maybe five minutes. Six at best. But it was plenty of time. The nine millimeter Parabellum traveled at 1,250 feet per second, much faster than the fastest cop car—hell, *any* car for that matter—and he was almost in perfect range now.

Then their eyes met.

Jimmy's face was a mask of maniacal horror and torn flesh, but his hand moved at blinding speed. John started to react, but a shot cracked the night, vaporizing the sirens for a moment, and John felt a punch in his gut. His free hand immediately moved from the graze on his side to a rapidly moistening spot low on the left side of his stomach. He glanced down and saw the blossom of crimson spreading and pouring through his fingers.

*Fucker shot me,* he thought in amazement. *He really sh—*

The sound of a door swinging open and smacking the side of the house caused him to look to his left, his face still frozen in stupefied awe. A large man in a black suit came rushing out of the side door of Jimmy's house, a large pistol in his hand. The man was covered in splinters and white dust, and his eyes were wild. Then a second man was rushing out, right behind him, similarly dressed and armed. The first man was raising his gun towards John, the second man aiming for Jimmy. From the corner of his eye, John could see Jimmy beginning to react, and John brought his Beretta up to the first man.

The man met his gaze, his gun almost up, teeth bared. John—still stupefied and frozen—instinctively squeezed the trigger, flashes of the junkie in the crack-house raising his hand to ward off the shots, of Tony telling them how he was planning to fuck them all and calling Jenny a bitch, all filling his mind.

He shot the man three times. He hadn't aimed, only reacted, but miraculously he hit him every time, center mass. The man flailed as he continued coming with his momentum, but then faltered and spilled to the ground.

At the same time, Jimmy had fired. John couldn't tell how many shots—he was too consumed with his own situation—but it was several. Blood, tissue, and brains showered as the two men collided hard with the earth, lifeless.

*What the fuck is going on?* John's mind raged.

Before he could formulate an answer, he heard Jimmy laughing.

"We've got ourselves a regular bloodbath here, Johnny!" he said insanely. "I guess there's room for one more."

John's eyes and mouth maintained their stupefied expression as he turned to face Jimmy, his hand still clutched to the wound in his gut. Jimmy was leaned against the ruined Subaru, raising the revolver up at John. The Beretta was still clutched in John's hand, but it hung at his side and he knew he didn't have a chance to get it up and fire in time.

"You and Jenny were supposed to be my family," he began, the faintest hint of pain in his voice. "Why the fuck would y'all do this to me?"

John began shaking his head, stupefied.

"We didn't do *anything* to you, Jimmy!" John screamed. "It was all Tony! I told you to stay off that shit, it has you all twisted up, not thinking straight. But you killed the only woman I ever loved, and I can't let that go."

Jimmy laughed again, shaking his head. "No, the chimp told me. You're a *liar!*"

He screamed this last part and John—wondering just what in hell Jimmy was raving about—saw him pulling the trigger. The hammer was moving back and there was just a split-second left in his life. John shut his eyes and conjured up a picture of Jenny, that morning coming out of the shower, naked and in love with him. Her smile, her warm voice. This was the image he wanted to carry with him into the great beyond, to whatever awaited him. It was her, at her happiest and most carefree, before all of this had spiraled out of control.

*Click.*

John heard the sound and his whole body jolted. The hammer had dropped. He was sure of it. It was a sound he'd heard plenty and it was unmistakable. But there was no shot. No boom. No more bullet holes in his body.

He opened his eyes and saw Jimmy looking at the revolver confused, a stupid and furious look on his face. Then he was pulling the trigger again. And again. And again.

*Click. Click. Click.*

The gun was empty. The shot at Tony's, the one which hit John's stomach, then the man on the lawn. He'd unloaded his gun and had nothing left to fire.

But John did. The Beretta held fifteen shots, and he still had most of them left. His face split in a grin of triumph and something akin to lust as he began to hobble toward Jimmy, dragging his wounded leg, gripping his bleeding stomach.

"Should've counted your shots, Jimmy!" he almost laughed as he heaved for breath, dragging himself closer. Jimmy was still dropping the hammer on empty rounds, fear finally spilling over his crazed face.

John reached him and took his blood-soaked hand off his gut, wrapped it around the base of Jimmy's neck, pulling his face towards them until their foreheads touched. He stuffed the barrel of the Beretta into Jimmy's solar-plexus, hard enough to make Jimmy cough.

"I loved you, you know that?" he asked Jimmy. "So did Jenny. We were brothers!"

John was hissing the words, spittle spraying on Jimmy's wide-eyed face. Sirens were wailing, closer now.

"God-damn you for this," John said.

He unloaded his gun into Jimmy.

Blood sprayed both their faces and Jimmy's body lurched with every shot, tears of horror and pain spilling down his blood-soaked cheeks. But John held on. Kept his hand at the base of Jimmy's neck and their foreheads pressed tightly against each other. He looked right into his friend's strained, insane, and terrified eyes as he pumped each round into him.

At last, the trigger quit moving. The slide was locked back, the magazine empty. Jimmy was groaning, blood spilling from his mouth, and he began to slide down the side of the car. John released his neck and stepped back, watching him go to the ground. Jimmy was trying to say something to him, his lips quivering and straining, but all that came out were cups of blood and a wet grunt.

A moment after he settled to the ground, he went still.

John stumbled back, dropping the pistol to the yard, and looked around. Every light was on, but no one was outside. Not yet anyway. The sirens continued to climb in volume, but they were still a few streets over.

He looked to the dead men on the lawn. One of them must have been the hitman Tony and his pal had set them up to rip off. He was amazed he and Jimmy could have survived them, but they had.

*Jimmy.*

His brother. They could have accomplished anything together.

Tears stung his eyes and he began to moan a scream. All the pain and anxiety of the past day overwhelming him all at once. And after all he had gone through, he was left with nothing and no one.

*Well...maybe not nothing.*

His eyes fell on the open trunk of the Subaru. Still weeping, sniffing back snot and wiping tears with his arm, he began to drag himself to the back of the car. Maybe there was still time. If he could move fast enough, maybe he could slip through the yards. Make his way back to Tony's. It was possible if he laid low. There were plenty of old sheds in this part of town. He could hole up overnight and through tomorrow if he had to and get back over there. Jimmy's car was there, keys probably in it. He always left his keys in it. And he could get Jenny, do right by her, and then vanish.

He got to the rear of the car and gazed down at the two bags. One of them was open, and he pushed the flap aside to take a glance inside.

There was a pistol.

*Tony's* pistol. Sitting right on top.

Then there was another of those unmistakable ratcheting clicks. Close by, too.

"John Savage, I presume?"

Antarctic winter seized him.

# Chapter 21

As John turned, he saw a third man—also in a black suit—standing about fifteen feet from him, a silenced weapon in his hand and an icy gleam in his eyes.

John's face seemed to sag. His right hand came up, gripping something invisible, and he whimpered as he remembered dropping the Beretta moments before. His hand fell limply back to his side and a gurgled cry or laugh—he wasn't sure which himself—escaped his lips with a trickle of blood. The man never flinched.

"John Savage, I presume?" the man repeated in a deep, grotesque voice. He was smiling, though so slightly and with such little humor John wasn't sure he could classify it as a smile at all. It was cold. Dark. Distant.

But it was also satisfied.

John stood as straight as he could manage on his good leg. His left hand dropped from his side, the pulsing blood flowing from his gut more freely now. Crimson soaked his jacket and shirt and pants. All of him, it seemed. It was wet and sticky and in places was beginning to dry and cake. His clothes clung to him and felt ready to split like wafers in some places.

A tear collected in his eye and suddenly, he was overwhelmed with a feeling of foolishness.

This is what it had all come down to.

Everything he'd planned, everything he'd done, it all came to this and nothing more.

*Was it worth it?*

The tear spilled over his blood-speckled face, mingling with the scarlet streaks, and finally dripped from his chin.

The man looked to the open trunk and nodded. The sirens were still wailing.

"Is that mine?" The man asked, though it wasn't much of a question. John actually managed to laugh.

"You're the guy, then," John said, a statement.

The man's gaze never wavered, and neither did the gun. The thick pipe of the silencer seemed to bore into him, mocking him.

The man nodded.

"That's right," the man said in a cold, even tone. "I'm the guy. Glad to have my property back. You guys fucked up. You know that, right?"

John managed a coughing laugh and nodded.

"I figured you did," the man went on, his smile widening the slightest bit. "Where are the others? You have a lady-friend, yes?"

John's eyes filled again with tears and he hitched and sobbed, spitting blood and spittle from his mouth.

"She's dead," he moaned. "They're all dead."

The man seemed to become disappointed all at once. His face clouded, not with anger, but resignation. As though some great loss had just occurred and he was letting it go, but not without some sadness.

John thought of Larry, then, and his family. Of Jenny on the floor of Tony's garage. Of Jimmy just a few feet away. Fresh tears flowed from him in rivers and he moaned a sob as he turned his head towards the trunk.

Towards the gun.

"Now, now," the man said, a mocking *tsk-tsk* tone to his voice. "Don't cry. You're a big boy. Sometimes even big boys make mistakes. Fuck up. You didn't know what you were getting into was all. I get it.

But this was all inevitable. I suppose there really is no honor among thieves."

John's grimacing face looked into the man's eyes with both horror and a sense of hope. Was the man going to leave him be? Leave him to whatever fate was waiting for him? Was it possible?

The man's smile faded and the coldness of his stare returned, turning John's already cold blood to ice.

No.

There was no mercy here. No reprieve.

This guy was having fun.

Sirens wailed louder still as John stared up at the man in the yard, cloaked in the gloom of the night.

"Let me get your money," John said and turned to the trunk. He reached in, grabbing one bag, but his hand hesitating over the other, preparing to dive in like a striking snake and grab the gun.

"Who *are* you?" John asked as he coughed once more. The sirens were deafening now. The police would be here in mere seconds.

The man in the suit smiled again, and his face took on a pleasant quality, as if two businessmen were meeting for the first time to discuss a new contract. It chilled John's blood even more.

"Call me Mr. Spears."

John nodded.

"Mr. Spears," he said. "It's been a god-damn pleasure."

His hand went for the gun. Wrapped around it. Came up with it. His finger was wrapping around the trigger and he was twisting his body towards the man, the one who'd murdered Larry and his family. He had the gun up now, nearly shoulder-level, his teeth snarling and bared like a feral animal. He was aware of a growling scream pushing itself through his clenched teeth.

There was a flash. And then, there was no more.

# Chapter 22

John's body sprawled to the ground, lifeless. There was no ceremony in it, only a jerk of the head, the blossoming flower of red, gray, and yellow as his brains exploded from his ruined skull, and a graceless collapse. The sound of the gun was a muffled *pop,* and nothing more.

Spears sniffed indifferently as he holstered his gun, then he snatched up the bags. After situating them on his shoulders, he ran from the yard in the direction he'd come, hopping over the dead bodies littered all about, and ran around the back of the house. He made his way silently through several neighboring yards, and moments later he was in his car, throwing the duffel bags into the back seat and dropping the transmission into gear.

He backed the car into the street, aware of the eyes watching as he sped away, but he wasn't worried about them. It was late, most of them were old, and he had a fresh set of plates to slap on as soon as he got out of here.

He sped down the street, his lights off, and turned at the first road he came to. As he did, he noticed the first red and blue lights flickering behind him. He was sure they hadn't seen him, but he was taking no chances. He accelerated and took every turn that came to him until he was on Highway 11 heading West, and he sped out of town. No one followed him. The din of the sirens had dimmed and faded as he went, and now, as he crossed the railroad tracks just out of town, they were gone completely. He took a nearby county road and found a thatch of woods he was able to pull his car into. He parked, got out, and cracked his neck.

*Damn, that was close.*

He pulled his lips back over his teeth revealing a devilish smile. He'd done it. All of Horowitz's crew was dead, and he had his money back. It was a shame about Vic and Paul, but that went with the business. They were expendable, anyway. He wasn't worried about any connection, because he and everyone he worked with had taken measures to be untraceable. Acid-burned fingerprints. Dentures. Fake IDs, or in the case of Vic and Paul, no IDs at all. There was *nothing* to trace back to him or his business, and he could rest easy knowing he and his clients were safe. You had to be safe in this business, or you didn't make it.

It was as simple as that.

He put the duffel bags in the trunk of his car, snatched the phony plates and put them on. Then he pulled up the GPS on his phone and followed backroads until he came out on Interstate 30 and headed back to Dallas. The drive was uneventful and there was not so much as a State Trooper in sight during the hour and a half stretch of freeway back to his home. All the problems were back there in podunk Winnsboro, and that was where they would stay, with the baffled local police and all the bodies left behind.

He got to his house, parked in the garage, and took his money inside. He returned it to his safe—a new one now, with a new code—and shut it away. He was home free.

Then, he went to sleep.

He awoke in the middle of the day. He was tired and had slept much longer than he'd intended to, but he felt he'd earned it. He made lunch and ate it alone at his kitchen table—a humble turkey and cheese sandwich with mayo—and watched the news on TV. Things were heating up in Syria again, and the President was bloviating about the patriotic duty of all Americans to dive into yet another civil war overseas.

His cell phone rang, and he snatched it up, muting the television.

"This is Spears."

"Alex," the voice on the other end said with a sigh, "we have a problem."

"What is it, Mr. Hays?" Spears asked. Hays was a client of his with a church in Longview, Texas which, contrary to its holy appearance, often required the services of Mr. Spears.

"I need you," J.R. Hays said. "There's a man we need found and dealt with. May have killed one of our girls from the place in Tyler."

Spears knew the place, he'd visited it often when he needed to get his dick wet.

"Who's missing?" he asked.

"Shari," Hays said.

"Fuck," Spears sighed. "I liked her."

"We all did," Hays went on. "Everyone did, as a matter of fact. Best pussy in East Texas. But that's not the issue. We need to find this guy, and fast. Can you bring Victor?"

Spears pursed his lips and shook his head in the empty room.

"Vic is out of service as of last night, I'm afraid."

Silence on the line for a moment, and then, "I'm sorry to hear that. Who do you have?"

"Doug is available. I'll call him. Where are we starting?"

"The motel the girl worked out of. You know the place, just outside of Tyler on I-20."

Spears knew the place. "Okay, it'll take me a couple of hours."

"Just hurry every chance you get," Hays said, his tone impatient. "You'll be meeting with John Elk. He runs the place. Goes by Johnny E. I think you've met him before."

"Yeah, I know who he is," Spears said. "I'll be in touch."

He ended the call, then called Douglas Weir. They arranged to meet and then Spears showered and dressed in another cheap, black suit. He loaded up his car with a change of clothes, some extra magazines for his pistol, and a bag of railroad spikes and hammers. Perhaps he'd get the chance to use them this time. He was still disappointed he hadn't gotten to use them on Horowitz's crew. It would have been nice.

*Oh, well.*

He was glad for the work. Keeping things regular. And it reminded him of why he did what he did. Because he was good at it. Because it felt good to be needed. To be the best.

To be your own boss.

Oh, friends and neighbors, Spears was good at his job. There were none better. He would find the asshole who nabbed Shari and deal out his chef's special with a wink and a wave. He could almost hear them screaming now, and he had to shift in his seat as his loins thickened.

He'd find them. He'd hunt them down like the dogs they were and deliver the goods. After all, that was his specialty. And there would be no more fuck ups. No sir. In, out, done. That was it. Nothing more, nothing less. Spears was the man for the job and the job was good. It was *so* good.

He smiled as he drove, his tobacco-stained teeth glistening in the afternoon sunlight. He found he was excited now. Looking forward to the job. To hunting down the dogs.

He looked forward to the hard goodbye.

If you enjoyed *The Hard Goodbye*, then check out *AND HELL FOLLOWED,* featuring "Behind Blue Eyes" by Chris Miller!

Made in United States
Orlando, FL
04 December 2022

25485571R00088